Pascoe Grenfell Hill

Life of Napoleon III.

SALZWASSER
VERLAG

Pascoe Grenfell Hill

Life of Napoleon III.

1st Edition | ISBN: 978-3-75250-285-5

Place of Publication: Frankfurt am Main, Germany

Year of Publication: 2020

Salzwasser Verlag GmbH, Germany.

Reprint of the original, first published in 1869.

LIFE

OF

NAPOLEON III.

BY

PASCOE GRENFELL HILL, R.N., B.A.

RECTOR OF S. EDMUND THE KING AND MARTYR.

" This is that joy in which my soul is strong,
That there is not a man among you all
Who can reproach me that I used my power
To do him an injustice . . . taking note
That I had not to do with easy times."—*Henry Taylor.*

LONDON:
EDWARD MOXON, SON & CO., DOVER STREET.
1869.

CONTENTS.

LIFE OF NAPOLEON III.

CHAPTER I.

EARLY YEARS AND EXILE.

1808—1838.

"*Je voudrais faire mieux connaître l'Empereur à votre nation :*" so writes M. l'Abbé Isidore Mullois, premier Chapelain de la maison de l'Empereur, in a letter now before me.—It is very well; but how can I contribute to make the Emperor better known to the British nation ? I cannot, —" as others use,"—compose a five-volume, or even a three-volume, work. A single sentence from the pen of M. Mullois re-assures me :— " *La brièveté* est aujourd'hui une des premières conditions du succès." A *short* summary, then, of the chief events in the career of Louis Napoleon may be acceptable to the English reader ; who will not forget that, while under former sovereigns all treaties of peace and amity between France and England have been false and hollow, our two nations throughout the reign of Napoleon III. have been true and fast allies both in peace and war. This we are bound to acknowledge with gratitude to the Almighty, " who hath taught us by His Holy Word that the hearts of kings are in His rule and governance."

Charles Louis Napoleon,* son of the King of Holland, Louis Bonaparte, and of Hortense Beauharnais, daughter of the Empress Josephine, was born at Paris, in the Palace of the Tuileries, on the 20th of April, 1808. His name was the first inscribed in the Imperial Register of successional rights, deposited in the archives of the senate. Only one other name was ever written in it : that of the King of Rome, born on the 20th of March, 1811. Of these two princes, heirs of royalty, and born amidst national rejoicings, one was destined to die at an early age, an exile from the land of his birth ; the other, preserved by Providence through many years of banishment or captivity, is now Emperor of the French.

"A letter addressed by Napoleon I. to Queen

---

* His name was put forth as " Louis Napoleon," at the election for the Presidency of the Republic, in 1848.

Hortense, during the infancy of the Prince, concludes with this sentence : *j'espère qu'il sera digne
des destinées qui l'attendent.*" More than thirty
years of trial and endurance were to elapse between
the expression of the above wish and the arrival
of him in whose favour it was formed at the
Imperial dignity. The political changes which,
during that interval, passed over the face of Europe,
afford matter for much variety of opinion. Few
will be inclined to dispute that, in England, the
public sentiment has undergone considerable
modification respecting the policy which resulted
in the treaties of 1815. And it is beyond all
controversy that, even at that epoch, the events
which have given it celebrity met, from minds of
keen penetration, a judgment wholly adverse to
that of their contemporaries generally. I will cite,
as an example, the single instance of Robert Hall,
whose high mental and moral qualifications are
universally acknowledged :—

"On the return of the Bourbons to France, a
gentleman called upon Mr. Hall, in the expectation that he would express himself in terms of the
utmost delight at that signal event. Mr. Hall said,
'I am sorry for it, sir. The cause of knowledge,

science, freedom, and pure religion on the Continent, will be thrown back half a century.' A few
years afterwards, on an allusion being made to the
battle of Waterloo, Mr. Hall remarked: 'That
battle and its results appeared to me to put back
the clock of the world six degrees.' "*

Hortense, who inherited from the Empress
Josephine a mild and amiable disposition, was also
endued with rare fortitude of character, which
the vicissitudes of her fortune afforded ample
occasion to display. France, after the disastrous
campaigns of 1814 and 1815, against the allied
powers of Europe, was in the occupation of
foreign armies; and the Napoleon dynasty lay
under the ban of a proscription which lasted
thirty-three years. Hortense and her children, ex-
pelled from their country, sought among strangers
a refuge almost everywhere denied. The Prince
Louis had at that time scarcely completed his
seventh year: it was with reason that he wrote,
not long since: "I was bred in the school of
adversity." Repulsed from the Grand-Duchy of
Baden; finding Savoy too insecure a residence;

---

* *Works of Robert Hall.* Edited by Olinthus Gregory,
Vol. vi. Appendix. Note A.

the fugitives took the road to Bavaria, where they obtained at length a resting-place for several years at Augsburg.

During their stay in that city the young princes were educated in exercises calculated to strengthen the faculties both of body and mind ; and it can scarcely be doubted that such early training tended to produce, in Louis Napoleon, the energy of character which has since surprised Europe. Already he gave proofs of that persevering application to the study of science and letters which he has continued through life.

In 1824, Hortense removed, with her children, from Bavaria into Switzerland, and purchased the Château of Arenenberg, in the Canton of Thurgau, or Thurgovia. This canton is situate in the valley of the Thun, and bounded towards the north by the lake of Constance and the river Rhine. Amid the solitudes of the Swiss lakes and mountains, the young Prince, during the opening years of manhood, nurtured the high aims and resolves which have, under Providence, raised him to so distinguished a rank among sovereigns. Here, too, he displayed that early predilection for the profession of arms which subsequent events have so eminently developed. In his library, books on military subjects held a chief place. The neighbouring camp at Thun, where the Swiss Republic assembles the militia of her various cantons, gave him an opportunity of making practical acquaintance with the details of the military art. One who knew him well at that time writes : " He applied himself with ardour to all parts of a soldier's duty ; toiling and faring as the private, working with spade and barrow; climbing, with a knapsack on his back, the steepest glaciers ; and the activity of his spirit led him to prefer always the most arduous adventure."

It was at the camp of Thun that intelligence reached the Prince of the Revolution at Paris, of July, 1830. The news brought to him at first a gleam of hope, as opening a prospect of return to his country. This hope, however, soon faded ; the proscription that hung over all who bore his name remaining as strict as ever. The National Assembly which raised the Duke of Orleans to the throne of France, and passed a decree banishing for ever all descendants of the elder branch of the Bourbons, appended to that decree a clause perpetuating equally the exclusion of all the Bonaparte family. In regard to Hortense, this sentence might seem the more harsh, inasmuch as, owing to her good offices, the first Emperor had not only permitted Louis Philippe's mother and her sister to reside in France, but accorded a considerable sum of money for their maintenance there.

In the autumn of 1830, many members of the Bonaparte family assembled at Rome, in order to confer on the change in the political aspect of affairs which had taken place on the Continent. To this conference Hortense repaired with her two sons. Their presence exciting some jealousy on the part of the Roman Government, the Prince Louis was, after a while, removed from the city, and rejoined his brother at Florence. Early in the year 1831 an insurrection of the Papal States broke out, and spread speedily through all the Legations. The brothers threw themselves with ardour into the movement : raised and organised bands of soldiers, and defeated those of the Pope in several slight encounters. The chiefs of the insurrection, however, through deficiency of military experience, committed the error of extending too much, instead of concentrating, the action of

their forces. Their successes were checked, and
the Vatican was relieved from its fears, by the
intervention of Austria, with assent of the French
Government. The elder of the two brothers,
Napoleon Louis, succumbed to an attack of internal
inflammation, at Forli, on the 27th of March, 1831.
Louis Napoleon, ill at Ancona, and in danger of
capture by the Austrians, who now occupied Italy,
was rescued by his mother, who hastened to his
aid, and, eluding the vigilance of the Austrian
police, succeeded in conveying him, disguised as
a domestic, to Cannes, in France, and thence,
towards the end of April, to Paris.

Their arrival in the capital caused so much
uneasiness, if not alarm, at the Court, and the
order issued for their departure, early in May, was
so peremptory, that Louis Napoleon, still suffering
from the effects of fever, was carried, wrapped in
blankets, beyond the gates of the city which he
has since done so much to improve and em-
bellish.

The exiles betook themselves to England, and,
after remaining there a few months, returned to
Arenenberg. Switzerland shewed her feeling in
regard to her guests by bestowing on the Prince

the honorary grade of citizen, and the rank of
captain of artillery in the regiment of Bern. On
his part, he testified his interest in the country of
his adoption by the publication of a pamphlet,
entitled : " *Considerations Politiques et Militaires sur
la Suisse:* " a work which brought its author into
communication with a master-spirit of his day,
Chateaubriand. Though chiefly of local interest,
the following passages, extracted from it, will
hardly need an excuse to the reader.

" CONSIDERATIONS ON THE CIVIL AND MILITARY POSITION OF SWITZERLAND.

" Previously to the French Revolution of 1789,
the Helvetian Republic, as we learn by the testimony of contemporary writers, underwent more
oppression from an aristocracy than even those
nations of Europe who were subject to monarchical
government. The privileges and the abuses of
power had reached, in Switzerland, their highest
point. There were sovereign cantons, and subject
cantons ; dominant cities, and subjugate provinces. The lands were placed under the control
of bailiffs (*land-voghts*), whose sway was arbitrary
and absolute.

" In 1798, when the French entered the territory, they abolished all those cantonal sovereignties; and established in their stead a single central power, similar to that which existed in France. Doubtless the French brought, together with the scourge of war, certain principles and systems, destined to develope themselves, at a later period, in a reconstruction of national strength and stability. But the temporary calamities incident on their invasion had so exasperated the minds of the people that they preferred a state of political subserviency to a liberty introduced by the hideous forms of violence and strife.

" In 1801, amid the various important events which took place in France, Napoleon alone, then First Consul, directed his attention to the condition of Switzerland. His wish was that the guardians of the Alps should frame a Constitution for themselves; and, by the Treaty of Luneville (9th February, 1801), he assured to them the right to adopt the kind of government which might best suit them. During the next three years the Swiss made trial of four or five different constitutions; while, in the disturbances that attended these changes, the old aristocratic principle still regained ground, at every step more and more menacing to the general liberty. . . The Helvetian Government solicited and obtained the intervention of Napoleon ; and, in consequence, the 'Act of Mediation' was signed, which, besides pacifying the rage of civil discord, conferred other important benefits on the country. It guaranteed the sovereignty of the people; abolished the predominance of one canton over another; and made of subjects fellow-citizens. The ' Act of Mediation '* was therefore a boon to Switzerland, for it healed her wounds and secured

* [The preamble to the "Acte de Médiation," written by Napoleon (November; 1802), is remarkably characteristic in its terseness and vigour of expression:—" Habitants de l'Helvétie. . . . Vous vous êtes disputés trois ans, sans vous entendre. Si l'on vous abandonne plus longtemps à vous-mêmes, vous vous tuerez trois ans, sans vous entendre davantage. Votre histoire prouve d'ailleurs que vos guerres intestines n'ont jamais pu se terminer que par l'intervention amicale de la France.

" Il est vrai que j'avais pris le parti de ne me mêler en rien de vos affaires ; j'avais vu constamment vos différents gouvernements me demander des conseils, et ne pas les suivre, et quelquefois abuser de mon nom selon leurs intérêts et leurs passions. Mais je ne puis ni ne dois rester insensible aux malheurs auxquels vous êtes en proie. Je reviens sur ma résolution. Je serai le médiateur de vos différends ; mais ma médiation sera efficace, telle qu'il convient au grand peuple au nom duquel je parle."]

her liberties.   From its date, until the year 1814, the Republic enjoyed uninterrupted internal tranquillity, in her alliance with France.

"But the disasters of Napoleon revived everywhere the dormant pretensions of the privileged classes.   Just as the Confederation of the Rhine abandoned its protector, so Switzerland, betrayed by her leaders, prostrated herself before the foreign sovereigns, to whom she hastened to open her gates.   The hordes of the North passed triumphant by the fields of Sempach and Morgarten. The trace which they left of their passage was the violation of those liberties which Napoleon had assured to Switzerland.   The aristocracy resumed its sway in the larger cantons ; the people lost their rights ; the union of all was weakened. Yes, it was in the name of liberty that the sovereigns dethroned Napoleon ; yet their victory was no less the triumph of aristocracy over democracy ; of legitimacy over the sovereignty of the people ; of privilege and oppression over equality and independence : the year 1815 was for Switzerland, as for so many other nations, a retrogression fatal to freedom.*

* " Une réaction liberticide."

"After the lapse of fifteen years, in July, 1830, France called to remembrance what she had lost, and what she might hope to regain. She arose,— and the noise made in bursting her fetters startled the nations from their slumbers. The country-men of William Tell, among the rest, recalled to mind that they had rights to vindicate. Switzer-land was indeed a republic, possessing the sem-blance of self-government, but, in reality, under the sway of the Holy Alliance. 'Our elections,' said its inhabitants, 'are not general; our press, not free; publicity denied in the courts of law, in the Legislative Council, in the Assembly of the Diet.'"

By the death of the King of Rome, which occurred at the palace of Schoenbrunn, in Austria, July 22, 1832, soon after the completion of his twenty-first year, Louis Napoleon became heir of the Emperor; and, after weighing the obliga-tions imposed by that title, prepared to vindicate the claims which he held it to confer. He was well informed, in his retirement, as to the state of affairs in France. Under the outward form of popular government, the Court maintained, in the representative chamber, a constant majority, through corrupt influences. The reigning family, treated with slight regard by the great European powers, sought to indemnify itself by unscrupulous intrigues for the aggrandisement of its own members. The army, turbulent and disaffected, vented its discontent in terms more military than elegant. From such symptoms the Prince foresaw and predicted that the downfall of the Orleans dynasty was inevitable.

The undertaking in which this conviction led him to embark has been generally condemned, and by no one more strongly than by himself, as premature, and having tended to compromise the welfare of France by plunging it into revolutionary commotion. Yet we, who know how little was required, but a few years later, to overthrow the throne of Louis Philippe, cannot pronounce the enterprise of Strasbourg, on the 30th of October, 1836, to have been so utterly wild and impracticable as at the time it was reputed to be. Its result was disastrous to those engaged in it. The troops whom the Prince first addressed, the 4th regiment of artillery, under command of Colonel Vaudrey, declared, indeed, in his favour, with shouts of " Vive Napoléon," and " Vive l'Empereur :" but this ardour was checked by adroit management of two other officers, who persuaded the garrison that they were imposed on by some mere pretender to the name of Napoleon. He was made prisoner ; conveyed, under charge of gendarmes, on the 11th of November, to Paris ; thence, after two hours' stay in the capital, to Lorient, in Brittany.

On the 21st of November the Prince sailed from that port, under an order from the French Government, for America : the intercession of his mother having obtained that he should not be put on his trial.

He wrote thus to her on the occasion : " I see, in the step that you have taken, all the tenderness of your affection. You have thought on the risk which I incurred, but you have not sufficiently considered my honour, which obliges me to share the lot of my companions in misfortune. It has grieved me much to abandon those whom I have drawn on to their ruin ; when my presence and testimony might have been of service to influence the jury in their favour. I have written to the King, entreating him to take a lenient view of their case."—They were set at liberty while Louis Napoleon was on his passage to New York.

Early in the following year, as he prepared to take a tour through the United States, the intelligence reached him of his mother's dangerous illness, which rendered necessary a severe surgical operation.—"If it should fail," she wrote to him, "receive in this letter my last blessing.—We shall meet, doubt it not, in a better world. In this, I leave little to regret but thy love, which has been to me the chief charm of life. To lessen thy sorrow, think that thy kindness and affection have made thy mother as happy as it was possible for her to be on earth. Think, too, of all my love for thee, and be comforted.—Above all, be assured that we shall meet again: that hope is too consoling, too necessary for us, not to be true. I press thee to my heart, my beloved!—I am quite calm, quite resigned: I trust that we may see each other yet once more even in this world.— The will of God be done!

"Thy tender mother,

"3rd April, 1837."   "HORTENSE.

On receipt of this letter, the Prince hastened back to Switzerland; and arrived at Arenenberg in time to receive her last farewell. A little while before the Queen expired she requested all the members of her household to be assembled in her chamber, that she might clasp each one by the hand. During a short delirium her words seemed to indicate that her mind wandered back to the last days of the Empire, and the scenes in which she had borne a part at Paris in 1815. She revived, to recognise those around her, made an effort to embrace her son, and breathed her last: (5th October, 1837.)

Shortly afterwards, the Government of Louis Philippe demanded the expulsion of Louis Napoleon from Switzerland. The gallant Republic refused compliance, and long negotiations ensued; the contention becoming at last so serious that France made preparation for war on her neighbour. This would have been an unmitigated calamity; to prevent which the Prince addressed, on the 22nd of September, a letter to the Swiss Diet, announcing his voluntary determination to withdraw from the country. In the following month he quitted Switzerland, and accepted the hospitality of Great Britain; landing on our shores on the 14th of October, 1838.

CHAPTER II.

CAPTIVITY AT HAM.

1840—1846.

PRINCE Louis Napoleon was received with sympathy in England, and met a hospitable welcome in aristocratic circles.   It will hardly be denied that he has, in return, shewn unvaryingly, by acts as well as words, a hearty and cordial desire to stand well with those whose friendship cheered his adversity.   During his residence at London (14th October, 1838, to 6th August, 1840) he did not intermit his habits of study ; spending frequently the morning from six o'clock till noon in literary labour.   Whatever else may be in question respecting him, there is one point at least on which the most sceptical will scarcely hint a doubt : the Emperor has been a hard student.   His " Life of Cæsar " is alone a sufficient proof to the world of that fact.   None need apprehend being accused of flattery in affirming it to be a work of extensive research, deep thought, and vigorous style.   I subjoin a list, though an incomplete one, of his earlier publications; premising only, as to the Manual of Artillery, that even in this day of recent improvement in that arm it is still cited as an authority, and that to its writer is due the germ of that terrific invention in modern warfare, the rifled cannon.

LIST OF WORKS.

Political Reflections . . . 1832
Considerations, &c., on Switzerland 1833
The Napoleonic Ideas. . . 1839
Historical Fragments . . . 1841
Analysis of the Sugar Question . 1842
The [projected] Nicaragua Canal . 1844
On the Extinction of Pauperism . 1844
Artillery Past and Future . . 1846

To notice all the productions of his pen that appeared from time to time in periodical publications would, to adopt a phrase usual in works of that class, "exceed our limits." The mention of a few titles may suffice to shew that they embraced topics of chief public interest in their day : " *The Slave Trade ;*" " *The Electoral System ;*" " *Military*

Organisation ;" "The Recruiting System in France ;"
" The Clergy and the State ;" &c., &c., &c.

Amid his literary occupations, the Prince turned
a watchful eye on the course of political events
across the channel, and the changes which seemed
impending in France. There were indeed in that
country statesmen, of high repute for sagacity, who
proclaimed loudly their confidence that the order
of things there established was fixed on as firm
a basis as human affairs can have, and as secure
from sudden and violent change. Thus M. Villemain, Minister of Public Instruction, on the 7th
of January, 1840, moving an address from the
Chamber of Deputies to King Louis Philippe,
concluded his speech in the following words :—

" During ten years France has sought, amid
all the perils of revolution, two inestimable bless-
ings ; a national dynasty, and a parliamentary
government. That dynasty, Sire, is your own :
that government is the one founded on the charter
of 1830. . . The cause of constitutional monarchy
may reckon on our faithful adherence. In vain
do insensate spirits yet meditate disturbance.
France guarantees that the efforts of faction shall
henceforth be powerless. The reason and the will

of the nation watch over the throne which they have erected; your rights are indissolubly linked with ours; and the glory of your crown adds to the greatness of our country."

Similar sentiments and principles were maintained by a still more distinguished advocate, M. Guizot. That they were not shared however by the nation generally, was indicated by a measure which followed, a few months later, for which no plausible motive can be assigned except the desire of conciliating popular favour. The same assembly which had voted the perpetual exclusion of the Napoleon family from France, now, with no slight vacillation, passed a decree that the body of the great Emperor should be brought, with the highest ceremonial honours, to its final resting-place at Paris. Various opinions have been expressed respecting the policy of Louis Philippe in sending his son, the Prince de Joinville, on such a mission. It would be of little use to inquire whether it was an act of royal policy or impolicy, or neither, but simply a concession to national feeling, which the will of the monarch would have been impotent to resist.

On the 12th of May, 1840, M. de Remusat,

Minister of the Interior, proposed to the French
Chamber of Deputies, amid general acclamations,
a measure for removing the mortal remains of the
Emperor Napoleon from the Island of St. Helena
to the banks of the Seine. The minister proceeded : " *Il fut Empereur et Roi : il fut souverain
légitime de notre pays.*"

The tribute thus rendered to his memory was accompanied by circumstances which could not but
be painful to all surviving members of his family.
A privilege was denied to them which is not refused to the poorest in the land, that of following
a relative to the grave. Napoleon I. was to be borne
to his tomb unattended by any of his lineage : and
his arms were delivered up to Louis Philippe.

Joseph Bonaparte, ex-king of Spain, made
an energetic remonstrance against the surrender
of Napoleon's sword to the Bourbons : and the
Prince Louis, while seconding the protest, in a
letter addressed to *The Times*, scarcely dissembles
his intention to push the matter beyond mere
words. " I concur," he writes, " in the protest
of my uncle Joseph, from the depth of my heart.
General Bertrand, in delivering up the arms of
the head of my family to King Louis Philippe,

has been the victim of a deplorable delusion. The
sword of Austerlitz should never be placed in the
hands of enemies to our house. They may expel
us from our country, confiscate our property, and
shew themselves generous only towards our dead :
all this we can endure, and without a murmur,
but to deprive the heirs of the Emperor of the
sole heritage which fortune has left them, is to
violate their most sacred rights, and force the
oppressed to say to the oppressor, at no distant
day: 'Render back that which you have usurped.'"

The irritated feelings of Louis Napoleon, at
this juncture, led him to undertake a second enterprise, which could not be justified either by sound
principle or policy; being calculated to retard,
instead of accelerating, the declaration of the
national will in his favour. The expedition to
Boulogne (6th August, 1840) although counting
among its adherents statesmen of capacity, as
Persigny ; warriors of experience, as Montholon ;
had never, from the outset, a prospect of success.
Its issue was even more disastrous than that of
the preceding attempt at Strasbourg. Two of the
Prince's friends fell at his side, and he was conveyed a prisoner, slightly wounded in the arm, to

the citadel at Boulogne. Shortly afterwards he was transferred, with the companions of his misadventure, to the fortress of Ham, near Saint Quentin, towards the Belgian frontier; and finally to Paris, where, with eighteen fellow prisoners, he was put on trial, on the 28th of September, before the Chamber of Peers.

The following passages are extracted from the speech of M. de Berryer, the eloquent counsel engaged for the defence of the accused :

" A minister of the king has lately declared, ' Napoleon was the lawful sovereign of our country.' And would you deny to this young prince,—rash, presumptuous, as you will, but marked by the high spirit of his race,—the right to say within himself: 'That name, which raises the hope of victory, and spreads the terror of defeat, is mine to bear to the frontier. I am the heir, the adopted son of the Emperor. This funeral procession which they prepare in his honour, it is mine to lead.'

" For, what do you pretend ? The arms that are to be placed on the tomb of the hero, do you dispute their possession with his heir ? Ah ! believe me, it was without premeditation that, young and ardent, the Prince exclaimed : ' I will go—I will head the train of mourners—I will place the sword of the Emperor on his tomb before assembled France.'

" If there was crime in this proceeding, the fault rests with you, who, by solemn acts of your Government, gave the provocation ; you, who decreed forfeiture of his rights, of his rank, even of his name and title as nephew of the Emperor ; while your very proscription tended to foster the conviction of those rights. If there has been a crime, it is you, I repeat, who have instigated it.

" And what will you do to him ? Will you hurl him afar to some desert rock, that a second tomb of Saint Helena may contain other illustrious relics ? Will you pronounce a sentence of degradation on him ? No ! an assembly of Frenchmen will never pass a sentence of degradation on *that* name.—It is impossible."

This speech, exhibiting perhaps some inflation of style, by license of forensic oratory, produced as little effect as probably was expected from it. The sentence passed on the Prince, on the 6th of October, was that of imprisonment for life in one of the fortresses of the kingdom.

He was taken back then to the old fort of Ham ;

having, as companions in captivity, Count Montholon, condemned to twenty years, and Dr. Conneau,* to five years, of detention. The future sovereign of the Tuileries was put in possession of three small barrack-rooms, in a very comfortless state of dilapidation. After some delay, the Government devoted about five and twenty pounds (600 francs) to the necessary repair of the apartments. Dignified and mild in demeanour, the Prince acquired the sympathy of all around him. The soldiers loved to watch him taking his daily walk on the terrace of the fortress, or cultivating his bit of garden. From time to time the cry of "Vive Napoléon!" would arise; and it was deemed prudent to make a frequent change of the troops in garrison.

The captive was also an object of interest to the inhabitants of the village of Ham, who came constantly at the hour of his walk, to salute him with their acclamations.

Among the graver employments of his prison hours was the composition of his "Extinction of Pauperism:" an inquiry into means for ameliorating the condition of the masses. He also sent

* Since physician-in-chief to the Emperor.

into the world from his prison the work entitled
"Analysis of the Sugar question," published in
1842, the object of which was to benefit the
agriculturist. When in after life a statesman
expressed to Louis Napoleon surprise at the extent
of the information possessed by him on many
various subjects, the reply was: "I studied six
years in the university of Ham." The Bishop of
Amiens, in whose diocese the fort is situated,
visited the captive; and, naturally, spoke words
of condolence. "Monseigneur," the Prince would
reply, "I thank you for your good and kind
words; but you must not think me too much to
be pitied. I have need of time and solitude, to
prepare me for the work to which I am destined
by Providence; for, prisoner though you see me, I
shall one day govern France." There appears no
reason to cast a shade of doubt on the sincerity
of that reliance on Providence which Napoleon III.
has unvaryingly professed, and which was so
strong as to communicate itself to the sharers in
his captivity. One of these, on being asked,
latterly: "Did not your days pass wearily in that
old fortress?" answered: "Not at all; we were
always with the Prince, and his conviction that he

should one day reign was so powerful that we all partook in it : we lived upon hope."

The imprisonment of Louis Napoleon had endured five years and nine months, when afflicting intelligence came to him from Italy. His aged father was dying, in the city of Florence, and wished, before his death, to embrace once more the only child that remained to him on the earth.

The Prince solicited permission to attend the death-bed of his father ; and offered his word of honour to return afterwards to his prison life. The Government of Louis Philippe refused to accede to his request unless on conditions impossible for him to accept. Then it was that, stung to the heart, he determined to escape, and proceeded to carry his design into effect with equal dexterity and success.

The chief agents in the enterprise were Charles Thélin, his faithful valet, and Dr. Conneau. Thélin having license occasionally to quit and to re-enter the citadel, it was arranged that he should ask permission from the governor to go to the neighbouring town of Saint Quentin, in order to purchase some necessary articles, and that, on his leaving the fort, the Prince should make his exit at the same time, in the diguise of a workman.

This plan offered two advantages: first, it would enable Thélin, who was to lead with him the Prince's dog *Ham*, to divert attention from the pretended workman, by the noisy gambols of the animal, a well-known favourite of the garrison: secondly, it gave Thélin an opportunity of calling to himself, on some ready pretext, any one who, believing the Prince to be really a workman, might be disposed to address him.

Monday, the 25th of May, 1846, was the day fixed on for carrying out the project. Louis Napoleon rose at a very early hour, and it is hardly necessary to say that his simple toilet preparations were speedily despatched. He put on first a suit of plain clothes, such as might be worn by a commercial traveller or clerk: over these, a blouse and pantaloons, much the worse for wear. A black wig, a shabby cap, and a blue apron, completed the costume. The time appointed for action now drew near, and he sat down to breakfast as composedly as on ordinary occasions. The repast over, he put a pair of *sabots* on his feet, and a short clay pipe, sufficiently black-ened with tobacco smoke, into his mouth; and, having remarked that the workmen, in passing to and fro, carried frequently planks on their shoulders, he drew out one of the shelves from his book-case, and so disposed it on his shoulder as to afford a screen, on occasion, for one side of his face.

At a quarter before seven, Thélin collected the workmen who were about, into an inner room, where he invited them to drink. Having effected this useful diversion, he hastened to inform the Prince that not a moment was to be lost. At the foot of the staircase leading from his apartments were stationed two guards, Dupin and Issalé by name. Thélin, to neutralise the vigilance of one at least, drew Issalé aside under pretence of hav-ing some interesting piece of intelligence to impart; and contrived to place him so that his back was turned to the next passer-by. The Prince now nimbly descended the stairs, holding his plank vertically, and directing its point straight at Dupin, so as to compel him to turn away his head, and prevent his observing features which he would too surely have recognised. In the court

beyond, a locksmith's apprentice, who followed
at a few steps behind, quickened his pace, in order
to overtake the supposed workman, with the apparent intention of speaking to him. Thélin,
however, called the lad and sent him back, on
some errand, to re-ascend the stairs.

It seemed next to an impossibility that the
prisoner, whose personal appearance had so long
been a subject of watchful observance to those
concerned in his safe keeping, and who had at
every few yards to encounter some one interested
in the detection of his disguise, should yet escape
discovery.

As he passed the first sentry, the Prince let his
pipe fall on the ground, and stooped, with much
deliberation, to pick it up and replace it in his
mouth ; the soldier meanwhile watching this pro-
cedure with a mechanical look of attention, and
then resuming his measured march. A little further
on was the canteen, by which the path lay to the
outer gate of the fortress. Here were groups of
soldiers, some on duty, some basking idly in the
sun. The officer of the guard was occupied in
reading a letter. The superintendent of the works
was likewise engaged in examination of papers,

and did not even lift an eye on the *workman* who brushed closely by him.

Between the inner and outer drawbridges of the citadel a greater risk of discovery occurred. Two carpenters approached the Prince, on the side which was unprotected by his plank; and, as they advanced, raised their voices in expressions of surprise at seeing one of their own calling at work there whom they did not know. The only expedient to which he could recur was to shift the position of his plank, as if tired of its weight, from one shoulder to the other, so as to intercept their view. They continued, however, to approach the object of their curiosity, till, when within a few yards, to his great relief, he heard one say to the other: *"Ah! c'est Berthoud."* Yes, " it was Berthoud: " so they thought; and this mistake of theirs saved him from the danger which threatened to overthrow his hopes of liberty on the verge of their fulfilment.

At the outer gate of the fort Thélin managed to attract to himself the notice of the porter. A sergeant of the guard fixed his glance steadily on the Prince, who bore the scrutiny without being disconcerted: the wicket was unbarred, and he passed from the walls of his prison into the open highway.

Here Louis Napoleon took at once the road to Saint Quentin, while Thélin went in a different direction to procure a carriage. At the first convenient opportunity, the Prince hid the plank, that had done him so good service, in a corn-field; threw his *sabots* into a ditch; discarded his blouse; and replaced his old cap by a smarter one edged with gold lace. Thélin soon overtook him with the carriage, and the five leagues to Saint Quentin were accomplished without impediment. Fresh horses having been obtained, the travellers proceeded safely to Valenciennes, where they arrived at half-past two in the afternoon. Here, for the first time, the passport question was raised, and Thélin exhibited one which he had received from an English courier. That of the Prince was not demanded.

To return now to the prison of Ham, and the events which were taking place there. Dr. Conneau had engaged to conceal as long as possible the flight of his friend. " My aim," writes the doctor, " was to secure him twenty-four hours' start of the orders that would be immediately issued on

D

his escape becoming known. I began by closing, with great care and caution, the door of his bed-room, wishing to give the impression that he was indisposed and must not be disturbed. In order to prolong the delusion to the uttermost, I placed between the bed-clothes a sort of *mannikin*, which I had dressed up, with its head—or the nearest resemblance to one that I could construct—disposed carefully on the pillow. In the adjoining room I kept up a very large fire, though the day was one of summer heat; thus raising the temperature of the apartment to a height suitable only for an invalid; all this to induce the belief that the illness of my patient was something serious.

" About eight o'clock some violet plants were brought by a messenger, whom I directed to prepare flower-pots with earth for their reception, but forbade him to enter the Prince's chamber.

" The commandant of the fort now called to inquire after the state of his health : and, about noon, made his second appearance.

" ' The Prince,' I said, ' is more calm.'

" Thus the day wore on smoothly, until, at a quarter-past seven in the evening, the worthy commandant entered the little ante-chamber in which I was seated, rather flurried in his manner, and with a look somewhat scared.

" ' Commandant,' I said, ' the Prince is going on favourably.'

" 'If he be really ill,' he cried, 'I must see him, I must speak to him.'

" On this I went into the bedroom and called the Prince by name, who *naturally* did not reply. I returned on tiptoe, my finger on my lips, as a sign that the patient was still asleep. The commandant could by no means comprehend to his satisfaction this prolonged slumber, and took a seat, saying : ' He is not going to sleep always ; I will wait here till he wakes.' Presently the evening drum beat, and the commandant started up. ' That must wake him, if anything will :' he cried, bending his body forward in a listening attitude. ' I think I hear him stir :' he added, entering the bedchamber.

' Oh ! for goodness sake,' I interposed, ' go no nearer ; you will be sorry if you do.'

" The commandant persisted in approaching close to the bed, where, to his amazement, he beheld—the *mannikin*.

" 'The Prince is gone,' said he, turning sharply round.

" ' Yes,'

" ' When did he go ?'

" ' At seven o'clock this morning.'

" At first the worthy officer seemed thunderstruck. I must do him the justice, however, to say that he never addressed a word of blame or reproach to me ; but, after the first shock, submitted, with the coolness of a veteran, to the blow which shattered all the hopes he might have entertained of promotion for eminent service.

" ' Well,' he remarked, ' a pretty trick you have played on me. But you have done your duty, and I have done mine, and will do it to the end.' So saying, he posted away, to give orders for immediate pursuit of the fugitives."

But they were already far beyond apprehension of re-capture. Having crossed the Belgian frontier, the path to Brussels was open to them. From Brussels, the prisoners of Ham passed to Ostend, and from Ostend to England.

CHAPTER III.

THE PRESIDENCY.

1848—1851.

LOUIS NAPOLEON, no longer a captive, was yet not free to take his intended journey into Italy. The Austrian ambassador at London would not be persuaded to sign his passport, and the Continental Powers of Europe, refusing him a passage through their territories, prevented his attendance at the deathbed of his father.

In England the Prince met as hearty a welcome as he had experienced during his former visit to our island. His mode of daily life too among us was, in all important points, unchanged, and such as to gain the respect and goodwill of those with whom he associated. Much of his time was applied to preparation for the press of works having in view objects of political interest and public utility. I have given, in a preceding chapter, some extracts from his earliest publication: *"Considérations Politiques et Militaires sur la Suisse."* It

seems not out of place to present here a short
specimen of the more matured powers of his pen,
in an essay entitled " *La Traite des Nègres.*"

" On the African Slave Trade.

" Honour to the philanthropist who, having
put forth a sublime and noble idea, directs it, by
a prudent application, to the benefit of the human
race ; but let us beware of the theorist who, more
showy than solid, pursues such an idea regardless
of adverse results, and, while embracing the world
in his schèmes of benevolence, inflicts injury on
his fellow-creatures.

" The distinctive characteristic of such persons
is to be passionately affected by sufferings the
most remote from them.   Their fervour augments
in direct proportion to the square of the distance
at which the object of their sympathy is placed.
Cold to the misery of the overworn French
labourer, who lives under the shadow of their own
roofs, let some tale of wrong reach them from the
antipodes, oh ! then all the feelings of the soul
are excited to the highest pitch.   Persons who
endure distress on the other side of the globe
appear far more worthy of compassion than those
who pine and languish in our native land.   Still

we would applaud and prize their exertions, if they tended to the good of any human being, since all men are brothers. Unhappily the effect is quite the contrary way.

" To take the facts of the case before us. The public sentiment of Europe was roused to indignation against slavery and the slave-trade. This sentiment, no less just than popular, has been seized on by would-be philanthropists, who aggravated the evil denounced, by the measures proposed for its remedy. And this is easy of proof. The burning plains of America are to a great extent cultivated by negroes. The African tribes are necessary to the climate; slavery compels them to labour; and their numbers are annually recruited by the slave-trade. A religious feeling, worthy of all praise, prompted Europe, moved by the woes of a whole race, to exclaim: 'Away with the slave trade! Away with slavery!'

" To this cry the European races who inhabit America responded : ' Emancipation is to us the synonym of pillage, ruin, death; for the slaves are our property, we have purchased them; if you would have their liberty, you must pay us its price; and, if you set them free all at once, they will murder us. We, as well as they, are your brothers, and claim equally your protection.'

" ' Be it so,' was the rejoinder ; 'let slavery then endure for the present, but abolish the traffic which adds constantly to the number of its victims ; let us have the right of search.' And what has been the consequence ? The slave-trade, being of imperative necessity to many parts of America while slavery exists there, must exist also. So long as the demand continues, it is impossible to exclude the supply. The slave-trade is carried on, on fully as large a scale as before, but as a contraband instead of a legal commerce. The wretched negroes, intead of being piled, scores upon scores, are now heaped, hundreds upon hundreds, in the slavers; and if a chase occur, many of them are thrown overboard, to evade the penalties affixed to the traffic by European Governments.

"In support of this statement, it may suffice to cite, out of a hundred cases, one that occurred on the coast of Brazil in 1836, and was well known to all the French squadron on that station. An English corvette, observing a vessel which bore all the appearance of a slaver, gave chase. The vessel in question, having made

all sail in order to escape, but in vain, as her
pursuer gained rapidly upon her, was seen to
throw overboard a large number of casks. One of
these floating near to the cruiser was hauled on
board, and, when opened on deck, was found to
contain a live negro ! It was the same with all
the other casks. Thus the laws of the philanthropists had the effect of converting slave-dealers into
murderers. Nor is the above an isolated instance.
It is stated that the number of slaves im-
ported annually into Brazil is greater now than
it was antecedently to the treaties for the suppres-
sion of the traffic. The right of search therefore
has rendered no service to the cause of humanity.
The negroes are far greater sufferers than before,
and so long as slavery itself exists the result will
be the same.

" What then remains to be done ? I answer, if
the question of the abolition of slavery had been
taken up by Governments wishing sincerely the
welfare both of the white and the black races,
they would have proceeded to train and prepare the
slaves in their colonies, by a gradual appren-
ticeship, for the transition from forced to free
labour. The Governments of Europe, thus acting

in concert, might have succeeded in persuading those of America to follow their example; whereas at present the Government of Brazil may ask France : 'By what right do you hinder me from importing slaves while you have slaves in your own colonies?'

"Slavery itself once destroyed, the slave-trade must of necessity perish by the same blow; and the claims of humanity would be satisfied. Whereas, up to the present day, while we are busy in sowing hatred between master and slave, the commerce in human flesh continues, and becomes all the more atrocious the more we attempt to repress it.

"Further, that very attempt supplies a ground of quarrel to England, who is ready to go to war for the right of search; and to sacrifice the lives of thousands of Englishmen and Frenchmen in the so-called interests of humanity.

"Let us repeat that, while a true clear-sighted philanthropy is among the noblest qualities of. human nature, so a false and perverted philanthropy is among the errors most detrimental to mankind.

"I cannot conclude better than in the noble

words of M. Villemain, uttered before he became a minister of State : ' *Il faut que la vérité soit une chose bien précieuse en ellemême ; puisque les erreurs généreuses des âmes pures sont presque aussi fatales à l'humanité que le crime, qui est une erreur des méchants.*' "

In the beginning of 1848, the political discontent, which had been constantly on the increase in France for several years, reached its highest point. It was founded mainly on two grounds : first, the narrowness of the electoral constituency, which restricted the privilege of voting to about one-tenth of the adult population ; secondly, the exorbitant amount of patronage held by the Court, which enabled it to command large majorities in the Chamber of Representatives. No rhetorical flourishes in the mouths of popular orators, vaunting the union of " Constitutional Monarchy and Parliamentary Government," could reconcile the nation to such a system, or retard its overthrow.*

* On the 10th of January, 1848, six weeks only before the deposition of the Bourbons, the Chamber of Peers voted an address to the King, which concluded in the following words : " In a Constitutional Monarchy, the union of the great powers of the State overcomes every obstacle, and guarantees the moral

On a sudden, a startling report rang through Europe. The throne of Louis Philippe had fallen, —fallen through its own inherent weakness, one scarce knew how,—and a republic was erected in its stead (24th February, 1848). The fact is that Louis Philippe and his dynasty had never taken root in the heart of France. He had been elected king *impromptu*, by some two or three hundred deputies, who professed to act " in the name of the nation," but who had no more commission to. proclaim a king than my courteous readers have to nominate a pope. The nation had never heartily confirmed the choice. At length the storm that had long been gathering burst forth in the revolution of February, and the Orleans monarchy vanished like " the fabric of a vision."

The moment seemed now to have arrived when Louis Napoleon, after so many years of exile, might hope to tread the soil of France as a free man. He hastened to Paris. The newly sprung

and material interests of the country. By that union, Sire, we will maintain social order in all its conditions. Our charter of 1830, transmitted by us to future generations as an inviolable deposit, will secure to them the most valuable inheritance which nations can receive, the alliance of order and liberty."

Provisional Government, consisting of Messrs. Ledru-Rollin, Lamartine, Louis Blanc, and others, shewed already signs of instinctive apprehension regarding him, and intimated that his presence might prove a " source of embarrassment" to them in the grand designs which they meditated. He accordingly returned to London.

The good-will and suffrages of his fellow-citizens followed him thither, when the tumult and confusion attendant on the outbreak of the revolution had in some degree subsided. His name, indeed, was unheard at the *general* elections for members of the National Assembly, holden on the 23rd and 24th of April. The Assembly was opened for its first sitting on the 5th of May. The *partial* or supplementary elections, caused by double returns or resignations, took place on the 4th of June following, when eleven new members were chosen for the Department of the Seine (Paris). The result was not officially known until the 8th of June; and the name of Louis Napoleon Bonaparte was little expected to appear in the list. The announcement of his election was received with shouts of enthusiasm by the crowds assembled at the Hotel de Ville. Simultaneously, the

Prince was chosen a representative of the people at the " *elections partielles* " for the Departments of the Yonne and the Charente-Inférieure ; and, on the 18th of the same month, for Corsica.

The official returns give the following figures :

" 4th June—Charente-Inférieure :

  Number of Voters 65,179

  Louis Napoleon Bonaparte 23,022 votes.

,, Seine—Number of Voters 248,392

  Louis Napoleon Bonaparte 84,420 votes.

,, Yonne—Number of Voters 57,571

  Louis Napoleon Bonaparte 14,621 votes.

18th—Corse—Number of Voters 39,330

  Louis Napoleon Bonaparte 37,036 votes."

Following close on the election of the Prince came the rumour of his expected entry into Paris.

One present at the time* records that, from the 10th to the 12th of June, " the people thronged the avenues to the Assembly, all pronouncing but one name, that of Louis Napoleon Bonaparte." On the other hand, the apprehensions of the republican party became now seriously aroused. On the 12th, on occasion of a sudden report of fire-arms near to the hall of assembly, M. de

* Lord Normanby.

Lamartine, springing to the parliamentary tribune, announced " *une occurrence fatale :*"—" the blood," said he, " which had never flowed in the pure cause of the republic, has now been shed on behalf of military fanaticism, for those shots have been fired with the cry of ' Vive Napoléon ! ' " The speaker therefore proposed that the Assembly should at once vote by acclamation the exclusion and exile of Louis Napoleon Bonaparte. This *coup-de-théâtre* of Lamartine produced an effect contrary to that which he intended, as it turned out that the firing heard was the accidental discharge of a pocket-pistol by a national guard, which had injured no one but himself. The discussion of the question relative to the exclusion of the Prince was adjourned to the following day, when his right to take his seat was affirmed by a very large majority. On the morning of the same day a telegraphic message had been written at the Ministry of the Interior, enjoining on all *préfets* and *sous-préfets*, throughout France, the arrest of the Prince :—" Le Ministre de l'Intérieur aux préfets et sous-préfets. Par ordre de la Commission du Pouvoir Exécutif faites arreter Charles Louis Napoléon Bonaparte, s'il est signalé, dans votre Département. Transmettez partout les ordres nécessaires."

On the 15th the President of the National Assembly read to its members a letter addressed to him on the previous day by Louis Napoleon :

"London, 14th June, 1848.

"M. le Président,

"On the point of departing to occupy my post, I learn that my election has been the pretext for deplorable errors and excesses. I never sought the honour of being a representative of the people ; knowing the unjust suspicions of which I am the object. Still less do I now seek power. *If the people impose duties on me, I shall know how to fulfil them.* But I disavow all those who would impute to me projects of ambition which I do not entertain. My name is a symbol of order, of nationality, of glory ; and it would be with the keenest regret that I should see it used to increase the troubles and distractions of my country.

"Have the goodness, M. le Président, to make this communication known to my colleagues.

"Receive the assurance of my distinguished consideration.

"Louis Napoleon Bonaparte."

A sentence in this letter, " *si le peuple m'impose des dévoirs, je saurai les remplir*," gave great offence to the Assembly ; who took it to imply ulterior views of an ambitious kind. General Cavaignac, who had rarely spoken except on topics connected with his profession, now added to the prevailing excitement caused by the reading of the above document. Rising in his place, he drew attention, with much warmth, to the circumstance that in the letter no reference was made to the Republic : " *le mot de la République n'y est jamais prononcé.*" " Upon this," writes Lord Normanby, who was a witness of the scene, " there arose such cries, there spread such universal agitation, as I had hardly ever before witnessed even within those walls." The storm thus raised was on the succeeding day (the 16th) quelled almost as suddenly, by a second letter, received by the President from the Prince, formally resigning his office of representative.

" London, 15th June.

" M. le Président,

" I was proud to have been elected representative of the people, at Paris, and at three other departments. It was, in my eyes, an ample com-

E

pensation for thirty years of exile and six of captivity. But the injurious suspicions to which my election has given rise, the disturbances of which it has been the pretext, the hostile spirit of the present executive power, compel me to forego an honour supposed to have been obtained through intrigue. I desire order, above all things, and the maintenance of a republic wise, powerful, intelligent; and since, involuntarily, I favour disorder, I place my resignation in your hands, not without deep regret.

" Receive the assurance of my distinguished consideration.

" LOUIS NAPOLEON BONAPARTE."

The feelings of the French people were more clearly pronounced in favour of the Prince, as the incapacity of the self-elected " Provisional" chiefs and the disastrous effects of their misrule became more and more oppressive. Tumultuous scenes and indecent altercations, of daily occurrence within the National Assembly, gave fresh impulse to the spirits of anarchy and disorder beyond its precinct. These broke out during the last week of June in a fierce insurrection, which overspread speedily the whole city of Paris.

A vivid description of the insurrection is given by two writers, most opposed to each other in general opinions, who were alike eye-witnesses of, and to some extent partakers in, the events which they narrate : the Marquis of Normanby (English ambassador at Paris), and " Citizen Louis Blanc." Without taking from either any statement at all of a controvertible character, we may accept their concurrent testimony as to the furious nature of the civil warfare which raged in the French metropolis.

" On Friday, the 23rd," writes M. Louis Blanc,* " a compact column, which had formed in the Place de la Bastille, fell like an avalanche on the Porte Saint Denis, where the first engagement took place. But already, whilst the National Guard were slowly assembling in the aristocratic quarters of the town, the populous streets bristled with barricades. . . .

" Whether the insurrection might not have been prevented from the first; whether barri-cades need have been left for boys to con-struct; whether, in short, General Cavaignac, by letting the insurrection pass, reserved to

* " Historical Revelations," by Louis Blanc.

himself the sinister honour of suppressing it,—
these are questions for History to solve. For the
present, I will only state this fact, that at four
o'clock in the afternoon, on the 23rd of June, in
the Faubourg St. Marceau, although it was in full
insurrection, the circulation was still free ; and
that it would have been perfectly easy for either
the civil or the military authorities to ascertain
that many of the barricades were guarded by men
incompletely armed, and utterly without ammu-
nition of any kind.

" The indomitable energy of the insurgents was
astounding. The regular troops and National
Guards fought well, as Frenchmen always fight ;
but those who were least liable to suspicion of
sympathy with the insurgents confessed that their
prodigious resolution and audacity would have
sufficed, under an able general, for the conquest of
the world ! Besides, thanks to M. Marie, the
atéliers nationaux had received a military organisation, and had been divided into brigades, squadrons, companies, comprising the men of the same
arrondissement, of the same quarter, of the same
street ; and, in a war of barricades, in which every
man resolved to fight and die at his own door, for

the bread of his own household, such an organisation lent a certain *ensemble* to the resistance, though the resistance was a local one.

"Overwhelming as the forces of the Government appeared, the end was still doubtful. In the Faubourg du Temple, where General Cavaignac had reconnoitred the fortresses, the fight assumed gigantic proportions. At the attack of the barricade Saint Maure, the troops suffered terrible loss, and were repulsed. When the darkness of night enveloped the streets, the insurgents were completely masters of that portion of the city.

"Terrible was the night, a night of expectation and grief! On the following morning [Saturday,] the heavy guns began to thunder against the Faubourg, without gaining the least advantage over the insurgents; while the troops advanced, retreated, and advanced again, with alternate wrath and discouragement. Until Sunday evening (the 25th) the blood of countrymen and fellow-citizens was flowing in disastrous rivalry. What was most lamentable of all was the inexorable fury of the fight between the working men and the Garde Mobile,—between fathers on one side and sons on the other. Everybody knows

now that, when the insurrection began, the Garde
Mobile was more disposed to join than to
attack the insurgents. But it had been so per-
tinaciously asserted that the insurrection was
against the Republic, that one more terrible
misunderstanding was added to the history of
civil conflicts.

"Let us pass to the Assembly. During all
these hours of devastation, the Assembly sat *en
permanence*, distracted by alternate hopes and
alarms. . . . Once, and once only, the whole
danger of the situation was laid bare with studied
exaggeration. This was when M. Pascal Duprat
proposed to declare a state of siege, and to confer
the dictatorship on General Cavaignac. 'No
dictatorship!' exclaimed M. Larabit, clinging to
the tribune, and demanding to be heard in the
midst of the uproar. M. Bastide came forward
and said : 'Make haste—in an hour the Hôtel de
Ville will be taken!' Thereupon the state of
siege is voted, and the dictatorship placed in the
hands of General Cavaignac. In the name of the
Republic, the subversion of all republican principles was voted by acclamation.

"I do but sketch the dark outline of this disastrous insurrection; but I may add a few details which will be found interesting.

"That night passed without any fresh attack by the troops; it was not until the following (Monday) morning, about eight or nine o'clock, that the Faubourg du Temple was completely invested. The insurgents beat a retreat, but did not cease to fire until they had expended their last cartridge. At five o'clock in the evening, La Villette was taken: that was the end of the bloody tragedy.

"An eye-witness assured me that, after that final struggle, a National Guard shot a man for the simple reason that he wore a red comforter round his throat.

"After the victory, the reprisals were terrible. Prisoners huddled together in the vaults beneath the terrace, in the garden of the Tuileries which faces the Seine, were shot at random through the air-holes in the wall: others were shot in masses in the Plaine de Grenelle; in the Cemetery of Mont Parnasse; in the quarries of Montmartre; in the Cloister of Saint Benoit; in the Court of the Hotel de Cluny. Wretched men whom General Cavaignac, in his proclamation of the 23rd of

June, had addressed in these words : ' Come to us, the Republic opens her arms to you : ' were dragged before councils of war, to be judged by the men they had fought : and the vanquished, whom General Cavaignac had promised not to treat as victims, were dispatched *en masse* without trial. In short, a horrible and humiliating terror spread over the devastated city for many days.

. . . " About 15,000 citizens were arrested after the events of June ; 4,348 were sentenced to transportation without trial, as a 'measure of general safety.' "

The narrative of Lord Normanby, differ as he might from M. Louis Blanc in his estimate of the causes which led to the " Insurrection of June," shews equally with the above its fierce and obstinate character. I proceed to make some extracts from his lordship's Journal, entitled : " A Year of Revolution."

" June 24, 1848. (Saturday).

" 8.30 A.M.

" I have just returned from the early morning sitting of the Assembly. The report made, upon the opening of the sitting, as to the events of the

night, was anything but re-assuring. There has
been a suspension of arms on the part of the
Government, apparently acquiesced in by the
insurgents, till after daybreak ; but the latter had
skilfully availed themselves of the interval in
strengthening many of their positions and multi-
plying their defences. There seemed to me intense
anxiety in the haggard looks of the deputies I
found there. It was at once proposed and carried
that Paris should be placed in a state of siege,
and all the executive powers given to General
Cavaignac alone. There having been some hesitation as to the mode of doing this, and much consequent tumult, M. Bastide obtained a moment's
silence, and appealed to their patriotic feelings,
adding : 'If you hesitate, in an hour the Hotel
de Ville may be taken.'

" 11.30 A.M. The attack upon the Hotel de
Ville has been repulsed ; but General Duvivier,
badly wounded, now calls loudly for reinforcements, or else he cannot answer for the result, if
the attack be renewed ; and indeed the insufficient
number of troops to deal with so vast an insurrection becomes everywhere apparent. . . It is said
that there never was such hard fighting in

France upon any former occasion of popular outbreak.

" 7 P.M. Some casualties, both of general
officers and of representatives, excite much sensa-
tion. Generals Bedeau and Dumesne are both
badly wounded. The latter, after taking the
Pantheon, which had for some time offered the
most desperate resistance, in an attempt to push
his advantage and carry a barricade behind it,
was shot in the leg and obliged to give up his
command to General Brea.

" 10 P.M. The President has just announced
that he has received a report from General Brea,
that the insurrection has ceased to exist on the
left bank of the Seine.

" June 25. (Sunday.)

" During the night the insurgents had gained
much ground ; had constructed many new barricades ; and, though driven from every position
on the south of the Seine, had occupied the whole
of the north-east of Paris, having their right at
Montmartre, and extending to the left over the
whole of the Faubourg Saint Antoine. . . The
Government express great confidence in the
certainty of the result, with the amount of forces

they have at their disposal; but the position occupied by the insurgents has been made so strong with barricades, and they possess so completely all the sympathies of those bad quarters, and therefore have every window in their favour, that there must still be a frightful loss of life, unless the Government have force enough to take the barricades also in the rear.

" The army have had a frightful loss of officers, as the marksmen from the windows almost always picked them out : but this has exasperated to the highest degree the soldiers of the line, who are determined to make a terrible example of those who still hold the barricades. Many persons of my acquaintance in society have suffered in the ranks of the National Guard, and some of the most respectable shopkeepers in Paris, known to all its frequenters as living in Rue de la Paix and the adjacent streets, have been killed. I trust that we may now anticipate the defeat of this attempt to establish a *République Rouge*. But peace, when restored to this unhappy city, will have been pur-chased at an awful price of human suffering and misery. To say nothing of the immediate ruin of hundreds of the middle classes, who were struggling against accumulating difficulties, and whom this blow will finish for ever, what is to become of the many thousands whose state, nearly approaching starvation, induced them to follow the counsels of desperate men ? Those who escape the immediate consequence of their guilt will find their condition more hopeless than ever.

"6 P.M. Last night I mentioned a report was read from General Brea, to the effect that the insurrection had been completely subdued on the left bank of the Seine. An account has now been brought to me which I cannot doubt is true, of his cruel and barbarous murder at the Barrière of Fontainebleau. Having imprudently yielded to an invitation on the part of these perfidious monsters to come within the enormous barricade .that was still garrisoned and defended by numbers, the General, over-anxious upon the instant to realize the assurance he had already given to the Government that the insurrection no longer existed in that part of the town, was induced to trust that, if he entered their fortified works, accompanied only by his aide-de-camp, they would be disposed to listen to him. Inveigled into a side-building, which they used as a head-quarter, they secured him and the officers of his staff, subjected him to every species of insult, and then murdered him in cold blood. When the barricade was carried by storm, he was found by the soldiers, who were much attached to him, not only dead, but a shapeless trunk; his arms, his legs, and lastly his head, having been cut off.

" June 26, (Monday), 1 P.M.

" If anything could have been rejected at once as incredible, it would have been that which I have just heard upon authority which marks it as indisputably true. The Archbishop of Paris, revered and beloved by all who knew him, had volunteered a charitable pilgrimage into the last stronghold of the insurgents, to stop, by his presence and influence, the further effusion of blood. The holy messenger of peace upon earth and good-will towards men has been slain,* by those who, it was found, had inscribed on their yet unfurled banners: ' *Vainqueurs, le pillage;— vaincus, l'incendie.*' "

It is to the credit of Lord Normanby's sagacity

* On Sunday, the 25th.

that he had foretold, previously to the outbreak of
June, the ruinous consequences which were to be
apprehended from the conduct of the men then in
power. Thus we read in his journal, under the
date of June 16 : " I have watched the conduct of
those who are now in power, for the last four
months. Whatever may be the exceptional qualities and personal distinctions of certain indivi-
duals, as a body of public men I believe that they
do not possess any one redeeming quality ; nor,
if they remain, could I foresee any other check or
limit to the mischief they are capable of doing
except their official incapacity and parliamentary
weakness."

The insurrection was subdued in the streets of
Paris, but discord presided within the National
Assembly : the various parties into which it was
divided, as legitimists, socialists, Orleanists, red
republicans, &c., &c., assailed one another with
still increasing acrimony and tumult. Meantime
the act of self-denial on the part of Louis Napoleon,
in resigning his post of representative, was far
from diminishing the public feeling in his favour.
The sort of persecution to which he had been
subject, from successive Governments, seemed

but to identify his cause still more with that of the people.

The 17th of September was the day fixed for the second set of " élections partielles," to supply the further vacancies caused by deaths, resignations, and double elections. The four departments which had previously returned the Prince re-elected him with largely increased majorities, and with the addition of another department, the Moselle.

" Elections Partielles of September, 1848. 17th September—Charente Inférieure :

Number of Voters 47,332
Louis Napoleon Bonaparte 39,820 votes.
,, Seine—Number of Voters 247,242
Louis Napoleon Bonaparte 110,752 votes.
,, Yonne—Number of Voters 50,445
Louis Napoleon Bonaparte 42,086 votes.
,, Corse—Number of Voters 32,968
Louis Napoleon Bonaparte 30,193 votes.
,, Moselle—Number of Voters 36,489
Louis Napoleon Bonaparte 17,813 votes."

It was now clear that the electors would allow no obstacle to interfere with the attainment of their object. Accordingly, at the sitting of the 26th of September, the President of the National Assembly proclaimed to its members the admission among them of " Citizen Louis Napoleon Bonaparte." On that day " he came quietly in at a side-door," writes Lord Normanby, " and took his seat (at first unperceived) on a back bench, during a dull speech, which his presence tended to shorten."

On the 5th of October, Louis Napoleon wrote to inform the President of the Assembly that, having been chosen by five Departments, he preferred to sit for Paris, as his birth-place.

The election of a President of the Republic, by universal suffrage, now approached. It was appointed to take place on the 10th of December; and, as the time drew near, it became apparent that no other candidate than the Prince had any chance of success. Not but that the struggle against him was severe. All the influence of the Government was employed; all arts were used by his opponents,—misrepresentation, calumny, and even ridicule,—to discredit his candidature. Such weapons, however, were without effect on the temper of the people. In all parts of France, far and near, the same spirit was manifested. The workmen in the cities pressed in crowds to record their votes in his favour. The impulse once given overthrew every impediment in its path. Men of wit and learning, political economists, and other philosophers, who dream that their vocation is to guide the course of the world, strove in vain to arrest the progress of the movement. The populations of the country were even more decided in sentiment than those of the towns. Everywhere the peasantry remained impassible to the arguments addressed to them : they listened to all that they were told, said little in reply, and took their own way. The result of the election was one to which the history of the world had presented no parallel. Nearly six millions of men, or, to give the exact figures, according to the official returns,—5,587,759,—placed the name of Louis Napoleon in the electoral urn. So that it may be said, without hyperbole, that he was borne to the supreme dignity of the State on the universal shout of France.

On the 20th of December, at an ordinary sitting of the Assembly, General Cavaignac resigned his temporary dictatorship, in a few appropriate words. The Prince-President, Louis Napoleon

F

Bonaparte, read an address of equal brevity. A great political transfer of authority was thus accomplished; and followed by an incident, very small in itself, yet worthy of note, as indicative of character in the persons concerned. " Louis Napoleon, after descending from the tribune at which he had read his address, walked to a back-bench where the General had retired, and in the most becoming manner held out his hand to him : Cavaignac took it, but never got up, and turned away his head to his next neighbour. There was mucn gentle kindness, and no ostentation, in the manner in which he approached Cavaignac, which contrasted favourably with the rudeness of the other." *

" Nations," it has been said, " have no gratitude." It is hard, however, to believe that the French nation, looking back to the state of their country immediately prior to the elevation of Louis Napoleon to the Presidency, can feel otherwise than deeply grateful for having been rescued from the sufferings to which they were a prey, and the worse calamities that threatened them. Industry languished in the cities for want of employ-

* " A Year of Revolution." Lord Normanby.

ment ; capital was banished by want of confidence ; commerce was extinguished; agriculture depressed under heavy imposts. The wages of the labourer were detained in the savings-banks (*caisses de retraite*) while national workshops were opened, in which men were paid for doing nothing. The press poured forth hideous publications, as the *Père Duchêne*, the *Journal de la Canaille*, titles revived from the reign of terror : and language was used at the clubs stimulating to the wildest excesses.

It is not pretended that the accession of the Prince to the Presidency of the Republic could at once remedy the ills of the country, and raise France to a state of prosperity. His path was beset by difficulties. During three years he strove with untiring energy to ameliorate the condition of society, and succeeded to a considerable extent in restoring peace, reviving confidence, and repressing the turbulence of demagogues. Still, his powers were limited by many restraints which checked his most earnest efforts for the public benefit. The "Red Republicans," as the party in the Assembly were called, attempted to thwart his measures at every step, and even muttered threats of impeachment against him. Those years of continued struggle (from December 1848 to December 1851) against the forces of anarchy, formed, we may well believe, not the least arduous portion of his career.

The state of parties in the National Assembly, towards the close of that period, is aptly described in a journal of the day, *Le Pouvoir*. It may be remarked that there was too much truth in the picture to please those who sat for it, and they in consequence inflicted on the journalist a fine of five thousand francs:

"It is a fact clear and evident, that order and tranquillity prevail far more outside of the National Assembly than within its walls. If there be a spot where strife and confusion reign triumphant, it is in the Legislative Sanctuary. What district is there, or what city, in which such furious menaces are hurled from one to another as in the Palace Bourbon? There is none; and, if any such could be found, much less would suffice to put that city or that district in a state of siege.

"Does any one suppose that a nation can go on with impunity feeding in itself a perpetual furnace of civil discord? We think not, and the history of the last sixty years is before our eyes, to shew us that, whenever our country has been set on flame, the torch has been applied by deliberative Assemblies.

" The Constituent Assembly was considered to have reached, in its fall, the utmost limit of degradation to which a deliberative body could descend; but the present Assembly appears determined to pass that limit and sink to a still lower depth.

" All its acts seem to be *premonitory of approaching dissolution.*"

CHAPTER IV.

THE COUP-D'ETAT.

December 2, 1851.

" Ye drive me close upon the rocks,
And of my cargo you're the vilest bales,
So overboard with you."

Philip van Artevelde, Act ii. Sc. 5.

PATIENCE, like all other human virtues, has its limits. The chaotic confusion of the National Assembly, as described at the conclusion of the foregoing chapter, was sufficient to exhaust the patience both of the nation and its Chief. On this point no better testimony can be desired than that given in the Assembly itself, by one of the most distinguished among its members, and one of the last who would be suspected of any undue leaning towards the Napoleon family. M. Montalambert in his speech of the 10th of February, 1851, said: " He did not come forward as the advocate or the friend of the President, but as a mere witness; and he declared with his hand on his heart, that Louis Napoleon had faithfully accomplished the mission he had received, of restoring society, re-establishing order, and re-pressing demagogues. The same men who now so violently attacked Louis Napoleon, placed themselves openly under his ægis after the 10th of December."

On the occasion of opening a railway from Dijon to Tonnerre, in the following May, the President of the Republic, at a banquet given in his honour at the Hotel de Ville of Dijon, declared: "The Assembly has given me its co-operation in every measure of repression, but has failed me in all the measures which I have devised for the welfare of the people."

Such a condition of things could not continue long. The rival factions in the State spent their time in little better than dissensions, intrigues, and recriminations,

"And of their vain contest appeared no end,"

unless civil warfare and national ruin. Each made in turn its advances to the Prince-Pre-sident; hoping, through alliance with him, to obtain a triumph over its antagonists. He lis-tened to their overtures, but forebore to connect himself with either of the parties, whose natural jealousies tended to paralyse the action of government.

Much has been said and written as to the "illegality" of the step taken by him to rescue France from ruin. It was surely a time for application of the principle : *Salus populi suprema lex esto.* France was a prey to the flame of civil discord, of which the National Assembly was the great central focus, when Louis Napoleon stepped forth, at considerable personal risk, to save the country. It must at least be confessed that the country was neither backward nor niggardly in acknowledging its obligations ; saluting him on all sides as its preserver, and applauding loudly the firmness and courage manifested by the President. Fortified by the adhesion of six millions of Frenchmen, who had given their suffrages in his favour, he resolved to make his appeal to the good sense, patriotism, and free will of the whole people.

The *coup-d'état*, if we may construe the act into words, with some familiarity of expression, spoke thus to the members of the Legislative Assembly : "Gentlemen, France suffers, and you pass your hours in talk. You will neither do any good yourselves, nor permit others to do any. And yet you are well paid for your attendance.* It is time to ask the French people, (the common master of us all,) whether it is its will that this abuse should continue or cease; to pronounce a verdict on your conduct and on mine."

The question thus raised was resolved on not a day too soon. His adversaries had already taken measures manifestly hostile to the office and person of the Prince. On the 5th of November, a day of note both in English and French Fasti, a bill (*projet-de-loi*) was passed which defined the process of impeaching the President of the Republic, and described the regulations to be observed on his trial :—" If the accusation be admitted, the National Assembly issues a decree convoking the High Court of Justice ; designates the town in which it will hold its sittings ; and nominates the Commissioners charged to conduct the prosecution. They enter immediately on the exercise of their duties. *The accused immediately ceases his functions.*" (Chap. iii. Art. 16.)

This was the last measure of any importance

* Each member received twenty-five francs *per diem*.

ever submitted to the Assembly. It would seem that, having accomplished this feat of legislation, they were content to repose for a while under their laurels. On the other hand, the Prince-President was not asleep. It may at least, without rashness, be assumed that he was fully awake on the night of the 1st of December ensuing; for on that night it was that he prepared the addresses to the French people, which, at day-break on the 2nd of December, 1851, met the eyes of the Parisians, covering the walls of their city.

"Appeal to the People.

" Frenchmen !

"The existing state of affairs can be endured no longer. Every passing day adds to the dangers which menace our country.

"The Assembly, which ought to be the firmest support of order, has become a hot-bed of sedition. Three hundred patriotic members have striven in vain to arrest its fatal tendencies. Instead of framing measures for the general interest, it forges weapons of civil war; it attacks the power which I hold directly from the people; it encourages every evil passion, and imperils the tranquillity of

France. I have dissolved it, and make the whole people judge between me and it.

"The Constitution,* as you are aware, was made with the object of weakening beforehand the powers which you entrusted to me. Six millions of votes† were a strong protest against it ; yet I have adhered strictly to all its provisions.

"Provocations, calumnies, outrages, have found me passive. But now that the basis of the compact is no longer respected by those who appeal to it so incessantly ; when the men who have already destroyed two monarchies would bind my hands, in order that they may subvert the Republic, it is my duty to frustrate their treacherous projects, maintain the Republic, and save the country by appealing to the sole sovereign whom I acknowledge in France, the People.

"I make, therefore, my loyal appeal to the whole nation, and I say : 'If it be your will that the present state of disturbance continue, choose another to fill my place, for I will no

---

* It was this Constitution, (voted by the National Assembly in November, 1848) of which the Duc de Broglie said : " C'est un œuvre qui a reculé les limites de la stupidité humaine."

† In December, 1848.

longer retain a power which is ineffectual for good, while it renders me responsible for acts of others beyond my control ; which ties me to the helm, while I see the ship drifting into the abyss.'

" If, on the contrary, you have still confidence in me, give me means to accomplish the grand mission which I hold from you.

" That mission is to close the era of revolutions, by satisfying the just wishes of the people, and protecting them from subversive passions. Above all, it consists in creating institutions which may survive their founders, and furnish at length the basis of something durable.

* * * * *

" Thus, for the first time since the year 1804, you will vote with a full cognizance of the cause, knowing for whom and for what. If I fail to obtain the majority of your votes, my duty will be to convoke a new Assembly, and surrender the office which I have received from you.

" If you are of opinion that the cause of which my name is the symbol, namely, France regenerated by the Revolution of '89, and organised by the Emperor, is still your own, proclaim it by ratifying the power which I ask.

" In that case, France and Europe will be preserved from anarchy, obstacles will be removed,
rivalries disappear ; for all will respect, in the
verdict of the people, the decree of Providence.

"LOUIS NAPOLEON BONAPARTE.

"December 2nd, 1851."

The plan of the *coup d' état* had been arranged
in all its details during the fifteen days immediately preceding it.   The President imparted his
views to but three persons : Marshal Saint
Arnaud, the Minister of War ; M. de Morny, a
representative of the people ; and M. de Maupas'
Prefect of Police. They all partook his sentiments
relative to the formidable and pressing danger
which menaced the whole fabric of society; and
they assured him at once of their utmost assist-
ance in support of the steps to be taken for repression of the evil.   De Morny undertook the
reponsibility of the political movement, as Minister
of the Interior ; Saint Arnaud, the conduct of the
military operations ; De Maupas, the action of
the police.   It was absolutely necessary to the
success of a scheme rarely equalled in difficulty,
boldness, and importance, that its principal
measures should be carried into effect nearly

at the same time : the arrest of the hostile party-leaders, civil and military ; the promulgation of the official appeals to the people ; the occupation of the House of Assembly, and distribution of troops at different points of the city, where their services might be required.

At eleven o'clock on the night of the 1st of December, the printers employed at the Government Press (*Imprimerie Nationale*) received a summons to attend at that establishment on an affair of urgency. As the bell tolled the hour of midnight, a company of gendarmes (*gendarmerie mobile*) under the immediate orders of Colonel de Beville, an officer of the staff of the President, arrived at the *Imprimerie* and took possession of the premises, allowing no one to enter or depart from them. These precautions taken, the printers were set at work on the documents required ; and the impressions when complete were conveyed to the office of the Prefect of Police.

Between three and four o'clock on the morning of the 2nd, forty commissaries of police, with a large number of picked men of that force, drawn gradually from different points during the night, were assembled at the Prefecture, and distributed

in detached groups in various parts of the building. They appear to have been under the impression that they were thus called together on account
of some plot which had been discovered among the
refugees in London. At five o'clock the commissaries descended one by one into the cabinet of
the Prefect, and there received from him, in a
very few words, full confidence as to the work
which they were required to perform. The arrests
were to be effected at a quarter after six, and the
police agents were to be at the doors of the
persons designated at five minutes after the hour.
All departed full of ardour to accomplish the task
assigned to them.

The persons marked for arrest and temporary
restraint were in total number, seventy-eight:
viz. eighteen representatives of the people (most
of whom were known to be engaged in conspiracy
against the authority of the President) and sixty
heads of secret societies, barricade chiefs, and ring-
leaders of the rabble, ready to execute the orders of
any faction for the sake of riot and plunder. It
was not to be expected that persons of either class
would submit to be disarmed and rendered innocuous
without offering every resistance in their power.

Curious and characteristic were several of the incidents which occurred in connection with these arrests. The most important of all, that of General Changarnier (Ex-Commander-in-Chief of the army of Paris,) was entrusted to two officers remarkable for energy, aided by fifteen men of the police, thirty of the republican guard, and ten cavalry. At five minutes past six punctually, the commissary rang the bell of the General's house, No. 3, Rue du Faubourg Saint Honoré. A voice from within asked : " *Qui est là ?* "

" *Ouvrez, on veut vous parler.* "

The porter was not, however, to be taken unawares, and refused to open the gate. The agent nearest to the wicket then received a whispered direction to hold the man in conversation, so to prevent his ascending the stairs to put his master on his guard, while the commissary found means of access for himself and his followers to the courtyard of the house through an adjoining shop. Immediately afterwards the sound of alarum-bells was heard, communicating with the bedroom of the General. At the same moment that the police entered his chamber, Changarnier opened the door of an inner apartment, and appeared *en chemise* and barefoot, holding a pistol in each hand. The commissary seized the weapons: "What do you mean, General? Do you defend your life before it is attacked?" On this, Changarnier gave up his pistols, saying: "I will dress myself, and be with you presently." In the carriage on the way to the prison Mazas,* he remarked: "The President was sure of being re-elected without a *coup-d'état*; he is taking a great deal of unnecessary trouble; when he gets himself involved in a foreign war, he will be glad to send for me to command his army."

The arrest of Cavaignac offered no graver obstacles than the foregoing. The commissary of police, having obtained admission into his residence, No. 17, Rue du Helder, inquired, "Which are the apartments occupied by General Cavaignac?"

"He is not at home," replied the porter.

"Oh! but I know that he is at home, and I must speak to him."

"But you call too early,—he is asleep."

A knock at the door of the General's bedroom drew forth the *question d'usage*, "*Qui est là?*"

* Near to the Pont d'Austerlitz.

G

" *Au nom de la loi, ouvrez.*"

" *Je n'ouvre pas.*"

" Then," said the commissary, " I will break into the room."

At this threat the General opened the door, and was greeted with the announcement: " You are my prisoner,—all resistance will be vain,—my measures are taken, in virtue of a warrant for your apprehension, which I will read to you."

Cavaignac here grew very excited, struck his fists violently on a marble table which happened to stand near him, and vented some highly abusive language. On being recommended to moderate his tone, he fixed his eyes keenly on the commissary:

" *You,—you* dare to arrest me? I will have your names."

" We have no wish to conceal them,—but that is not our present affair. Will you be so good as to dress yourself, and accompany us ? "

On the way Cavaignac appeared plunged in deep reflection; interrupted only once, to put the question: " Am I the only person arrested ? "

" General, I have no information to communicate on that point."

LIFE OF NAPOLEON III. 83

" Whither, then, are you conveying me ? "

" To Mazas."

General Bedeau occupied a large mansion, 50, Rue de l'Université. He was at first as one struck dumb by the unexpected and early visit of the police ; but, recovering himself, began to declaim loudly against their " violation of the law and the constitution."

" Take notice," he said, " that I am a representative of the people, vice-president of the Assembly ; a soldier, too, of the Republic, who have shed my blood and risked my life in its cause."

The commissary replied that he also was prepared, on his part, to sacrifice his life in the discharge of duty ;—that he was there not to discuss his orders, but to perform them.

At the last, General Bedeau, persisting obstinately in the refusal to quit his chamber, was carried out by force, vociferating : " Treason ! To arms ! See how they treat a representative of the people. They dare to lay hands on the vice-president of the National Assembly ! " At the prison, he attempted to harangue a company of the *garde républicaine*, who turned a deaf ear to him.

Charles Lagrange, residing at 27, Rue Casimir

G 2

Perier, was awakened by shrill cries of a female servant, startled at seeing her master's domicile invaded by an armed force. After having protested against the compulsion used, he submitted to it with military coolness; remarking, several times: " *Le coup est hardi, mais c'est bien joué.*" " A bold stroke, but well played." On arriving at the prison, he met Lamoricière, and said : " Eh, bien! mon géneral, nous voulions le mettre dedans; mais c'est lui qui nous y met :—*ma foi! c'est bien joué!* "

M. Greppo, the noted socialist, who lodged at No. 15, Rue de Ponthieu, was found to have a little arsenal of arms and munitions of war beneath his bolster : a huge battle-axe, freshly sharpened ; two daggers ; a loaded pistol ; and a superb *bonnet rouge,* or cap of liberty, quite new. Notwithstanding such martial preparations, the abrupt entry of the police completely prostrated M. Greppo. Mdme. Greppo, evidently a woman of stronger mind than her husband, exerted herself, in animated terms, to raise his drooping courage : " Is it possible," the lady asked, " that a man can have so little resolution as to let himself be taken without resistance ? " " How could he resist ? "

asked a spectator of the scene : " M. Greppo was seized by a (bodily) derangement,* over which he had no control."

When the commissary of police entered the chamber of M. Thiers, that statesman was fast asleep. On being aroused, he started up in a sitting posture, and, drawing aside the curtains of crimson damask, lined with white muslin, inquired what was the matter.

" I am come to perform a duty, and to make a search : but be composed, no violence is intended to your person."

This assurance was very much needed by M. Thiers, who was in a state of great trepidation. " What are you going to do," he asked : " do you know that I am a representative of the people ? "

" Yes, I am aware of that fact ; but I have only to execute the orders which I have received."

" But the act in which you are engaged may conduct you to the scaffold."

" Nothing shall deter me from the performance of my duty."

" But this is a *coup-d'état.*"

* "Monsieur Greppo fut saisi d'un dérangement auquel il dut satisfaire."—Granier de Cassagnac.

" Monsieur, I have no instruction to debate these questions with you ; and your intelligence on such subjects is doubtless far superior to mine. Pray have the goodness to rise and perform your toilet."

No papers of any political importance were found in the apartment of M. Thiers; which he accounted for by saying that, for several years past, he had transmitted all documents of such a kind to England. He shewed signs of much anxiety at quitting his house ; and, on arrival at the prison, all firmness forsook him. By the will of the President, and out of regard due to the eminent historian of the Consulate and the Empire, M. Thiers was released from further restraint, permitted to return, provisionally, to his own house, and, six days afterwards (8th December), conducted to Germany.

While the above persons were arrested, others, of far more dangerous character, were also seized without difficulty in their beds, and placed in safe custody. These were members of secret seditious clubs and societies, the daring implacable enemies of all order, whose main objects were pillage and massacre.

By a combination between the prefect of police and the minister of war, these arrests were arranged to precede by a quarter of an hour the arrival of the troops at their appointed stations.

At half past six precisely, M. de Morny, with an escort of 250 chasseurs de Vincennes, established himself at the *Ministère d l'Intérieur*, conveying thither to M. de Thorigny a letter of thanks for his past valuable services, and informing him, on the part of the President, of the decisive course on which he had resolved.

At the same time a company of the 42nd regiment of the line, under command of Colonel Espinasse, had obtained full possession of the Chamber of Assembly. A number of representatives, who, hearing of the arrest of their colleagues, hastened to the chamber, found its doors guarded by soldiery, who repelled them at the point of the bayonet.

At seven o'clock, the addresses to the people, which had been prepared during the night, issued from the prefecture of the police : the "Appeal to the French people" (already given at page 74); a Decree abolishing the Assembly; and the following "Proclamation to the Army :"

" Soldiers,

" Be proud of your mission. You will save the country ; for it is on you that I rely, not to violate the laws, but to enforce the supreme law of all, the national sovereignty, of which I am the legal representative.

" You have long suffered, like me, from obstacles raised to hinder both the measures which I would have carried out for your benefit, and the demonstrations that you wished to make in my favour. Those obstacles are overthrown. The Assembly has ceased to impugn the authority conferred on me by the whole nation,—has ceased to exist.

" I appeal now fairly to the people and to the army, and I say to them : ' Either give me the power to do that which your interest requires, or choose another to fill my place.'

" In 1830, as in 1848, you were treated like a conquered people. After having branded your heroic disinterestedness, they disdained to ask your votes or to consult your wishes. You are, nevertheless, the flower of the nation. Now, at this solemn crisis, it is my desire that the army make its voice heard.

" Vote, then, with freedom, as citizens ; but

forget not, as soldiers, that implicit obedience to the orders of the Head of the Government is the strict duty of the army, from the general to the private. It is for me, who am responsible for my actions before the people and before posterity, to take such measures as seem indispensable for the public good.

" On your part, remain firm and unshaken within the rules of discipline and honour. By your imposing attitude, protect the country in a calm deliberate declaration of its will. Be ready to repress every attempt against the free exercise of the sovereignty of the people.

" Soldiers! I speak not to you of the recollections which my name excites. They are engraven on your hearts. Your history is mine : we have been companions in the past in glory and suffering : in the future we shall be associated in aim and purpose for the repose and grandeur of France.

" LOUIS NAPOLEON BONAPARTE.

" Palace of the Elysée,
   2nd December, 1851."

The response of the army to this address was enthusiastic and unanimous. At ten o'clock on the morning of the 2nd, the President, mounting his horse, traversed the ranks of his troops, to the shout, a thousand times repeated, of " *Vive Napoléon!* "

About one o'clock in the afternoon, some two hundred deputies, belonging chiefly to the Legitimist and Orleanist parties, assembled at the *mairie* of the 10th *arrondissement*, presided over by two of their late vice-presidents. They proceeded to vote the President of the Republic " guilty of high treason," and " deprived of all authority." This decree, though passed by fewer than one-third in number of the ex-representatives, was supported by plentiful harangues. " There were," writes an auditor, " speeches in the room, speeches outside in the court, speeches from the windows, speeches from the tables, speeches from chairs."

M. de Morny, meanwhile, hearing of these proceedings, thought proper to put a stop to them. By his direction, General Forey despatched a company of *chasseurs-à-pied*, accompanied by a strong force of police; whose arrival on the scene produced a speedy change in the aspect of affairs. The soldiers, headed by their officers, sword in hand, appeared at the door of the apartment.

After a pause, the vice-president, Benoist-d'Azy, addressed them as having come to receive orders from the meeting, informed them of the decree which had just passed, and bade them retire. On this, the commissaries of police entered the apartment, and stated that they were come, not to place themselves under the orders of the Assembly, but to take into custody all its members who refused to disperse at once. Benoist-d'Azy replied : " We are here the sole representatives of law and right. We will not disperse, nor will we leave this chamber except under constraint. Seize us and convey us to prison." " All, all," exclaimed the other members. After considerable expostulation, without any effect, the commissaries, in order to bring matters to an issue, took the two vice-presidents by the collar, and led them off. The whole body then rose and followed, arm-in-arm, two-and-two, across the city, to the barracks of the Quai d'Orsay, where they were shut up for the night.

It would have been unreasonable to expect that the *coup-d'état* could be accomplished without encountering opposition. Such opposition, however, was in no degree that of the people. The honest industrious working classes were all in favour of the movement, and returned, in heart and voice, a general echo to the words of Lagrange: "*c'est bien joué.*" Blood indeed was shed, and lives were sacrificed in civil conflict; a frightful calamity under any circumstances, though, on this occasion, far less in extent than some persons, for purposes of their own, have been willing to represent it.

On the 4th of December, the President published a decree calling on the people to exercise the right of universal suffrage, and declare whether they would entrust to him the power to frame a new constitution. By the terms of this decree, "every Frenchman aged twenty-one years, and in enjoyment of his civil and political privileges, is called to vote: the suffrage to take place by secret ballot, by "yes" or "no," by a voting-paper, either written or printed."*

On the same day a lamentable event occurred in the boulevards of Paris. Armed agitators and

---

* A few days later (8th December) the President issued another proclamation to the French people, in which this sentence occurs: "If I have not your confidence, if your ideas are changed, there is no need to shed precious blood: you have but to place in the urn a contrary vote."

demagogues, among whom were members of the
late Assembly, carrying drawn swords, had
mingled with the lowest class of the populace,
inciting them to insurrection. Barricades of formidable description were raised, and desperately
defended; though carried at last by the valour of
the troops, not without considerable loss of life
on both sides.

The conduct of the soldiers, in the trying circumstances under which they were placed on this
occasion, has been highly praised by some, and
by others as sharply condemned. It is stated that
shots were fired on them from windows and balconies, overlooking the principal barricade, and
that they retaliated without discriminating the
particular houses from which the shots proceeded,
so that the innocent suffered with the guilty.
Deplorable indeed it is that a single innocent life
should have been thus sacrificed: it will scarcely
be pretended, however, that the blood of soldiers
shed in the fulfilment of their duty is less precious than that of other persons. It appears from
every account that the acts of the insurgents were
plainly those of men whose object was plunder
and violence ; and that the French nation at large

sympathised with the army in its stern repression
of the marauders.]

It would be useless, however, to attempt to
bring into harmony the violently conflicting
opinions which have been expressed respecting
the conduct of the President and his adherents at
the crisis in question. I would rather recur to
the testimony of the same illustrious French
royalist whom I cited at the commencement of
this chapter as an unimpeachable witness. M. de
Montalembert, in a letter which appeared in the
Univers, thus states the grounds of the vote
which he intends to give in favour of the President, in response to his appeal to the nation:
" To vote against Louis Napoleon would be to
declare in favour of a socialist revolution, the only
thing which can at present succeed the existing
Government. It would be to call the dictatorship
of the Reds to displace the dictatorship of a Prince
who has, during the last three years, rendered in-
comparable service to the cause of order and of
Catholicism. It would be,—taking the hypothesis
most favourable and least probable,—to re-estab-
lish the Babel known by the name of the National
Assembly, and which would certainly be power-

less in the formidable crisis that now prevails.

" But to vote for Louis Napoleon is not to approve of all that he has done : it is to choose between him and the total ruin of France. It is not to say that his government is that which we prefer to every other : it is simply to say that we prefer a prince who has given such proofs of resolution and ability to those persons who are now shewing their principles of murder and pillage. It is to arm the temporal power, the only power at present possible, with the force necessary to put down the army of crime, and protect our churches, our hearths, our wives and daughters, from the greed and violence of those who respect nothing. If Louis Napoleon were a man unknown, I would undoubtedly hesitate to confer on him such a power and such a responsibility : but I seek in vain elsewhere for a system able to guarantee to us the preservation and development of the benefits which marked his government. I see only the gaping gulf of victorious socialism."

It may here be remarked, as one of the earliest and most striking proofs of reviving public confidence, through the events of the 2nd of December, that the five per cent. stock, which on the 1st of December stood at 91fr. 60c., rose by steady advance to 100fr. 90c. on the 16th of the same month. In other words, the wealth of the nation, public and private, received in a fortnight an increase of nearly one-tenth.

On the 20th and 21st of December the balloting took place, throughout France, on the proposition submitted to the nation for its acceptance or rejection : " The French people wills the maintenance of the authority of Louis Napoleon Bonaparte, and delegates to him the powers necessary to frame a constitution."

The nation answered in the affirmative by the voices of seven and a half millions of men. A consultative commission, composed of former representatives of the people, under the presidency M. Baroche, waited on Louis Napoleon, at the Palace of the Elysée, at eight o'clock on the evening of the 31st December, 1851, to report officially the result of the ballot.

Ayes	.	.	7,473,431
Noes	.	.	641,351

The Prince then addressed the members of the commission as follows :—

" France has responded to my frank appeal, and has recognised that I have in no instance departed from the law except to restore right. More than seven millions of votes have just pronounced an indemnity and justification of an act which had no other object than to spare France, and probably Europe, years of trouble and calamity. I thank you for having stated officially the extent to which this manifestation has been national and spontaneous.

" If I congratulate myself on this immense adhesion, it is not through pride, but because it assures me freedom to speak and act as becomes the chief of a great nation like ours.

" I appreciate all the greatness of my mission, nor do I dissemble its grave difficulties. But with a heart right, and with the concurrence of all good men, who, like yourselves, will aid me with their intelligence, and support me by their patriotism; with the tried devotedness of our brave army; above all, with that Divine protection, the continuance of which it is my intention, on the morrow, solemnly to invoke ; I trust to render myself worthy of the confidence which the people still repose in me. I trust to secure the pros-

H

perity of France, by establishing institutions which may correspond alike to the democratic instincts of the nation, and to the desire universally expressed for a strong and respected Government.

"In effect, to meet the exigencies of the time by a system reconstructive of authority, without wounding the principle of equality, without closing any door to improvement, will be to lay the foundations of the only edifice capable of upholding hereafter a wise and beneficent liberty."

CHAPTER V.

The Empire proclaimed at Paris.

2nd December, 1852.

At the commencement of the year 1852, the Prince President, supported firmly by the voice of the people, was free to pursue the plans which he had formed for the re-establishment of peace and social order. France, too, breathed freely, delivered from the ruin into which the rage and tumult of civil discord had been precipitating her. On the 14th of January, Louis Napoleon promulgated a new Constitution.

"Preamble of the Constitution.

"Palace of the Tuileries, 14th January, 1852.

" Louis Napoleon, President of the Republic.

" Frenchmen,

" When, in my proclamation of the 2nd of December, I expressed to you frankly, according to my view, the vital conditions of power in France, I was far from pretending, as is so common in our days, to substitute the private theory of an individual for the experience of ages. On the contrary, I sought, in exploring the past, to discern the examples best worthy of imitation; the men who had furnished, and the benefits which had followed, them.

" Thus, I held it reasonable to prefer the precepts of genius to the specious dogmas of men of abstract ideas. I took for a model the political institutions which, at the commencement of this century, under circumstances nearly similar to the present, supported the tottering fabric of society, and raised France to a high pitch of prosperity and greatness. I took for a model institutions which, instead of vanishing at the first breath of popular clamour, succumbed only to the force of combined Europe arrayed against us. In a word, I said within myself : ' Since France, for the last fifty years, has moved and had her being in virtue of the administrative, military, judicial, financial, religious, organisations of the Consulate and the Empire, why not adopt also the political institutions of that epoch? Issue of the same mind, they should partake the same impress of nationality and practical utility.'

" In effect, as I recalled to you in my proclamation, our actual condition of society (it is important to state the fact plainly) is no other than
France regenerated by the revolution of 1789, and
re-organised by the Emperor. There remains
nothing of the ancient régime but great recollections and great benefits : all that was then organised was destroyed by the revolution ; and all
that has been organised since, and exists still, is
the work of Napoleon. 　 * 　 * 　 *

" We may affirm, then, that the frame of our
social edifice is the work of the Emperor ; and
has survived his fall, and three revolutions. Why
should not *political* institutions which had the
same origin have equal durability ? My conviction on the point has been long formed ; and I
therefore submit to your judgment the principal
bases of a Constitution taken from that of the
year VIII. Approved by you, they will become
the foundation of our political Constitution.

" Let us examine their spirit.

" In our country, during a monarchial era of
eight hundred years, the central power has been
constantly acquiring strength. Royalty crushed
the great vassals ; revolutions themselves removed

hindrances to the speedy and uniform exercise of authority. In this country of centralization, public opinion has incessantly referred all matters to the chief of the State, whether for good or ill. To write, therefore, at the head of a charter, that such chief is irresponsible, is to thwart public sentiment, and set up a fiction thrice swept away already amid the din of revolutions.

" The present Constitution, on the contrary, proclaims that the Chief whom you have chosen is responsible to you : that he retains at all times the right of appeal to your sovereign judgment, to the end that, on grave occasions, you may either withdraw or confirm your confidence in him.

" Being thus responsible, it is but just that his right of action should be free and unfettered. Hence the necessity that his ministers, able and valuable auxiliaries to his thought, should no longer form a responsible council, a solid knot of colleagues, a daily obstacle to the direct will of the Chief of the State ; the expression, too, of a policy emanating from the Chambers, and thereby subject to frequent variations, which render impossible all continuous purpose, all application of a regular system.

"Nevertheless, the higher placed, the more independent a man is, and the greater the confidence reposed in him by the people, the more his need of faithful and enlightened counsels. Hence the creation of a Council of State, to be in future a true council of government, first wheel in the machinery of our new organisation; composed of men of proved ability, engaged in framing measures of law in special committees; discussing them afterwards in general assembly, with closed doors, without oratorical display; and, finally, presenting them to the acceptance of the Legislative Body.

"Thus, power is free in its movement, enlightened in its progress.

"We have next to consider the control exercised by the Chambers.

"One Chamber, which takes the name of the Legislative Body, passes laws and imposes taxes. Its members are chosen by universal suffrage, singly, not by list; the people thus electing their representatives separately, will the more readily appreciate the merits of each. This Chamber will not number more than about two hundred and sixty deputies. Thus a first security will be

afforded for calmness in debate ; since we have
but too often seen the ardour and agitation of the
passions increase in an assembly in proportion to
the number of its members.

" The report of their proceedings, published for
the information of the nation, will no longer be
entrusted, as heretofore, to the party-spirit of
different journals : one report only will be allowed,
published under the official authority of the
President of the Chamber.

" The Legislative Body discusses freely the
measures laid before it ; adopts or rejects them ;
but without the power of extemporising amendments, such as derange frequently the whole eco-
nomy of a system, and defeat its main object.
Still less does this Chamber possess the initiative
of parliamentary measures ; a source of grave
abuses, permitting any private member to obstruct
all the proposals of Government, and present in
their stead the most crude and shallow projects.

" Another Assembly takes the name of Senate.
It will be composed of such elements as, in every
country, exercise a legitimate influence : talent,
fortune, an illustrious name, public services. The
Senate is not, as the Chamber of Peers was, a pale

reflex of the Chamber of Deputies : repeating the
same discussions, after the lapse of a few days, in
another tone. It is the depository of the national
compact, and of constitutional liberty; and it is
in reference solely to the great principles on which
our social condition is based that the Senate
examines the laws, and proposes new ones to the
Executive power. It intervenes to resolve any
grave difficulty which may arise, in absence of the
Legislative Body ; to explain the text of the Constitution, and enforce its provisions ; to annul all
illegal and arbitrary acts.   *   *   *

" The Senate will not be, as the Chamber of
Peers was, transformed into a court of justice, but
will preserve its character of supreme moderator ;
since political bodies always lose favour where the
legislative sanctuary is converted into a criminal
tribunal. The impartiality of the judge is too
often called in question, and he suffers in
popular opinion, which goes sometimes so far
as to deem him the instrument of party malice
and hate. A high court of justice, selected
from the chief magistracy, having for jurors
members of the councils-general throughout
France, will alone repress attacks upon the

Chief of the Government and the safety of the public.

" The Emperor told his Council of State : ' *A Constitution is the work of time ; one cannot leave too large a margin for improvements.*' And thus our present Constitution has fixed nothing absolutely except that which it was impossible to leave unsettled. It has not circumscribed by an impassable line the destinies of a great people ; but has left sufficient room for changes to allow, in a time of crisis, other means of preservation than the disastrous expedient of revolution.

" The Senate has the power, in conjunction with the Government, of modifying all but the essential parts of the Constitution. As to its primary bases, sanctioned by your suffrages, no change can take effect until it have received your assent.

" Such are the ideas, such the principles which I am authorised by you to carry into force. May this Constitution give calm and prosperous days to our country ! May it prevent the return of those intestine conflicts in which victory, however justly won, is always dearly purchased ! May the sanction which you have given to my efforts receive the blessing of Heaven ! *Then* peace will be

assured at home and abroad, then will my wishes
be fulfilled, my mission accomplished!

"LOUIS NAPOLEON BONAPARTE."

"CONSTITUTION

" Made in virtue of powers delegated by the French
p3ople to Louis Napoleon Bonaparte, by vote of
20th and 21st December, 1851.

" I.

" Art. 1. The Constitution recognises, confirms,
and guarantees, the great principles proclaimed in
1789, as the foundation of the public rights of
Frenchmen.

" II. THE GOVERNMENT OF THE REPUBLIC.

" Art. 2. The Government of the French Republic* is confided for ten years to the Prince
Louis Napoleon Bonaparte, the present President
of the Republic.

" Art. 3. The President of the Republic governs
through the medium of Ministers, a Council of
State, the Senate, and the Legislative Body.

* [Many of these articles necessarily underwent considerable modifications, consequent on the re-establishment of the
Empire.]

"Art. 4. The Legislative power is exercised by the President of the Republic, the Senate, and the Legislative Body.

"III. The President of the Republic.

"Art. 5. The President of the Republic is re-, sponsible to the French people; to whom he has at all times the right of appeal.

"Art. 6. The President of the Republic is the Chief of the State, and commander of the military and naval forces; he declares war, concludes treaties of peace, alliance, and commerce; nominates to all offices, issues regulations and decrees necessary for the execution of the laws.

"Art. 7. Justice is administered in his name.

"Art. 8. He alone initiates laws.

"Art. 9. He has the prerogative of pardon.

"Art. 10. He sanctions and promulgates the laws, and the acts of the Senate.

"Art. 11. He represents annually, by a message to the Senate and the Legislative Body, the state of affairs within the Republic.

"Art. 12. He has the right to declare any department or departments in a state of siege; under proviso of reporting the case to the Senate with the least possible delay. The consequences resulting from a state of siege are regulated by law.

" Art. 13. The Ministers depend solely on the Chief of the State. They are not responsible, except each in his particular department, for the action of Government : they have no conjoint authority. The Senate alone is empowered to place them under accusation.

" Art. 14. The Ministers, the members of the Senate, of the Legislative Body, and of the Council of State ; the officers of the army and navy ; the magistrates, and all public function-aries ; take the following oath : 'I swear to be obedient to the Constitution, and faithful to the President.'

" Art. 15. A vote of the Senate shall fix the sum payable annually to the President.

*   *   *   *   *

" IV. The Senate.

" Art. 19. The number of the senators shall not exceed one hundred and fifty : for the current year, it is fixed at eighty.

" Art. 20. The Senate is composed : 1st, of the

cardinals, marshals, and admirals ; 2nd, of citizens whom the President may judge proper to elevate to the senatorial dignity.

" Art. 21. The senators are irremovable and for life.

" Art. 22. The senators perform their functions gratuitously; the President of the Republic may, however, grant to members of the Senate, in consideration of their services and circumstances of private fortune, a yearly pension not exceeding thirty thousand francs.

" Art. 23. The President and the Vice-presidents of the Senate are nominated by the President of the Republic, and selected from among the senators. They are appointed from year to year. The salary of the President of the Senate is fixed by a decree.

" Art. 24. The President of the Republic convokes and prorogues the Senate ; and fixes the duration of its sessions by a decree. Its sittings are not public.

" Art. 25. The Senate is the guardian of the national compact and of the public liberties. No law can be promulgated without having been submitted to it.

" Art. 26. The Senate will oppose the promulgation : 1st, of laws contrary and hostile to the Constitution, to religion or morality, to the freedom of worship, to individual liberty, to equality of citizens before the law, to the rights of property, to the independence of the magistracy ; 2nd, of laws which might tend to compromise the safety of our territory.

* * * * * *

" V. THE LEGISLATIVE BODY.

" Art. 34. Its election takes place on the basis of population.

" Art. 35. There shall be one deputy to the Legislative Body for every thirty-five thousand electors.

" Art. 36. The deputies are chosen by universal suffrage ; and singly, not by list.*

" Art. 37. They receive no payment.

" Art. 38. They are elected for six years.

" Art. 39. The Legislative Body discusses and votes laws and imposts.

" Art. 40. Every amendment adopted by the committees charged to examine projects of law,

* " Sans scrutin de liste."

shall be sent back by the President of the Legislative Body to the Council of State. Unless approved by the Council of State, the amendment cannot be submitted to deliberation in the Legislative Body.

" Art. 41. The ordinary sessions of the Legislative Body last three months ; its sittings are public, but, at the request of five members, it may resolve itself into a secret committee.

" Art. 42.* The reports of the proceedings of the Legislative Body, whether in the journals or in any other channel of publication, shall consist merely of the minutes drawn up at the close of each sitting, under direction of the President of the Chamber.

" Art. 43. The President and Vice-presidents of the Legislative Body are nominated by the President of the Republic for one year; and selected from among the deputies. The salary of the President of the Legislative Body is fixed by a decree.

" Art. 44. The Ministers cannot be members of the Legislative Body.

* This article was modified by an Act of Government, 2nd February, 1861.

" Art. 45. The right of petition is exercised only towards the Senate : no petition can be addressed to the Legislative Body.

" Art. 46. The President of the Republic convokes, adjourns, prorogues, dissolves the Legislative Body. In case of dissolution, the President of the Republic is bound to call another within the term of six months.

" VI. THE COUNCIL OF STATE.

" Art. 47. The number of counsellors of State, for ordinary service, is from forty to fifty.

" Art. 48. They are nominated by the President of the Republic, and removable by him.

" Art. 49. The Council of State is presided over by the President of the Republic, or, in his absence, by the person whom he may designate as Vice-president of the Council of State.

" Art. 50. The Council of State is charged, under direction of the President of the Republic, with the preparation of projects of law and the regulations of public administration : also, with the solution of any difficulties which may arise in matters of administration.

" Art. 51. The Council of State, on the part of

I

the Government, maintains discussion on projects of law, before the Senate and the Legislative Body. The President of the Republic designates those counsellors who are to speak in the name of the Government.

" Art. 52. The salary of each counsellor of State is twenty-five thousand francs.

" Art. 53. The Ministers have place, rank, and voice in deliberation in the Council of State.

" VII. THE HIGH COURT OF JUSTICE.

" Art. 54. A High Court of Justice will judge, without appeal or suit for reversal (*sans appel ni recours en cassation*) all persons accused of crimes, conspiracies, attempts, against the President of the Republic or the security internal and external of the State. It can be convened only by virtue of a decree from the President of the Republic.

" Art. 55. The organisation of this high court shall be determined by the Senate.

*   *   *

" LOUIS NAPOLEON.

"Palace of the Tuileries,
14*th January*, 1852.

" Keeper of the Seals,
" Minister of Justice,
" E. ROUHER."

It would scarcely be profitable to notice the various comments of which the above Constitution has been the subject. It is apparent to all that under its working France has, by favour of Providence, advanced in wealth and prosperity, and has attained her present pitch of honour and eminence in Europe. Among the more important modifications which the Constitution of January 1852 has received in later years are : free publication of the debates, both in the Senate and the Legislative Body ; admission of the Ministers, *ex-officio*, to seats in the Chambers, and the right of questioning them there ; extension of the privilege of amendments to the Legislative Body ; relinquishment, on the part of the Chief of the State, of the power of opening supplementary or extraordinary credits during the prorogation of the Chambers ; finally, the liberty of the press and the right of public meeting.

The abolition of the National Assembly by Louis Napoleon, on the plea that it spent its time in talking instead of working,—a reproach, it must be confessed, not entirely peculiar to that body, but laid sometimes to the charge of deliberative assemblies in other countries,—implied a pledge that he would proceed on a different course, and substitute deeds for words. In redeeming this pledge, his efforts were especially directed to the relief and benefit of the poor and suffering classes. In evidence of this, it will suffice to mention the bare titles (not regarding closely the order of date) of various laws originated and institutions founded by him :

1. Law for improving the dwellings of the working classes.
2. Loan Societies. (*Institution de Crédit Foncier.*)
3. *Societés de Secours Mutuels,* or Mutual Aid Societies, to make provision for their members in sickness, and for their widows and orphans.
4. Retiring Fund for the poorer assistant clergy (*les desservans les plus pauvres.*)
5. Asylum for Incurables at Vesinet.
6. Convalescent Institution at Vincennes.
7. Refuges for Old Age.
8. Orphanages.
9. Maternity Societies : to provide attendance on poor women at their houses, during childbirth.
10. Organisation of public baths and lavatories.

Among the decrees issued by the President, there is one for the observance of Sunday rest in all public works. The French clergy attest that the example set by the Government on this point has exercised a degree of salutary effect towards the repression of labour on the Lord's day throughout the land.

It is note-worthy that Louis Napoleon did not confine himself to devising measures of utility to the public, but lent also in many cases the aid of his own personal direction and supervision. To take a single instance : in the heart of France, situate between Orleans, Bourges, and Blois, there existed a large extent of barren and almost desert territory, called La Sologne. Its condition, surrounded on all sides by fertile lands, had long been a scandal to the nation, and a source of misery to the wretched inhabitants of the district. On the 21st of April the President repaired thither in person, to examine for himself into the evil, and to apply if possible an efficacious remedy. I give the result in the words of M. Mullois: " Le Président, après avoir tout examiné, distribue de l'argent, de bons conseils, et de bons exemples : des canaux sont creusés, des routes sont tracées :

le pays se transforme de jour en jour, et l'on voit les plus belles récoltes remplacer la bruyère ou des touffes d'un bois chétif. La santé et l'aisance remplacent la fièvre et la misère."

The *plébiscite* of December, 1851, some account of which has been given in the preceding chapter, had extended by a term of ten years the period for which the Prince was elected to the Presidency of the Republic. The word " Republic " has, however, but little charm for the French people; to whom it recalls too sad images of woe and crime.

On the other hand, "The Empire " is a name associated with many a high and honourable recollection dear to the mind of every Frenchman. " *Nous voulons un Empire !* "   " *Il nous faut un Empereur !* "   " *Vive Napoléon Empereur !* " Such were the cries which met the ear in the capital and were re-echoed from the remotest corners of the country.

On the 14th of September, 1852, the Prince commenced a journey through the provincial parts of France, which afforded a full opportunity to verify the dispositions of the people towards him. In the towns through which he passed, multitudes assembled to see him from many leagues round, and, in default of hotels, bivouacked in the public squares. On all sides Imperial emblems and inscriptions appeared, as " Ave, Cæsar Imperator." " At every point of my passage, from Paris to Lyons," said the President, in an address to the inhabitants of the latter city, " the cry of ' Vive L'Empereur ' has been raised."

In his speech to the Bordeaux Chamber of Commerce, on the 9th of October, he thus sums up the impressions made on him in the course of his journey :—

" Its object," he said, " as you know, was to acquaint myself by personal observation with our beautiful provinces, and to investigate their wants. It has given rise, however, to a result far more important.

" In fact, and I say it with a candour as far removed from pride as from false modesty, never has any people manifested more plainly, more spontaneously, more unanimously, its desire to free itself from solicitude as to the future by concentrating the power that concerns it into one and the same hand. It is that the nation now knows the fallacy of the hopes by which it has been deluded, and the reality of the dangers that menaced it.   It knows that, in 1852, society was rushing to its ruin, each party consoling itself beforehand for the general shipwreck, in the hope of planting its own banner on the floating fragments.   It bears me good will for having saved the vessel by uplifting only the banner of France.

"Disabused of absurd theories, the people have acquired the conviction that those pretended reformers were mere dreamers; for there was always disproportion and inconsistency between the means at their disposal and the results which they promised.   The nation now surrounds me with its sympathies because I am not of the tribe of ideologists.   That which the country requires is, not the application of any new-fangled system, but, above all, confidence in the present, security for the future.

"And for this reason France desires a return to the Empire.

"There is, however, one apprehension which I feel bound to allay.   Certain persons in a spirit of mistrust, say: 'The Empire is war.' I say, on the contrary: ' The Empire is peace ! ' It is peace, because France wishes it, and when France is satisfied the world is tranquil.

" Glory is indeed transmissive by inheritance, but not so war. Have the Princes who valued themselves, and justly, on being grandchildren of Louis XIV. recommenced his wars ? War is not waged for pleasure, but from necessity, and, at the present epoch of transition, when by the side of so many elements of prosperity there spring so many causes of death, it may well be said : woe to the man who shall first give to Europe the signal of a collision, the consequences of which none could calculate.

" Yet I admit that I have, as the Emperor had, many conquests to achieve. I have, like him, to win over to peace and reconciliation rival factions ; and to bring back into the main popular current the hostile derivatives which now lose themselves without profit to any.

" I would recover to religion, to virtue, to comfort, that part of our populations which in a land of faith and belief scarcely knows the precepts of Christ ; and, in the bosom of the most fertile country in the world, hardly enjoys the first necessaries of existence.

"We have immense uncultivated tracts to reclaim, roads to open, harbours to clear, rivers to render navigable, canals to finish, our network of railways to complete. Opposite to Marseilles there is a vast kingdom to be assimilated to France. There remains yet to be organised a system of steam communication which may approximate all the great commercial ports on our western coast to the continent of America. In a word, we have on every side ruins to repair, false gods to overthrow, truths to make triumph.

"Such is my idea of an empire, if an empire we are to have.

"Such are the conquests to which I aspire; and all you who surround me, all who desire with me the welfare or our common country, you are my soldiers."

Louis Napoleon came back to Paris about the middle of October, having been absent just a month. The preparations made to celebrate his return to the capital were on the most magnificent scale; and he re-entered the city amid acclamations of many hundred thousand voices, and cries of " Vive l'Empereur! "

The voting for the Empire commenced on the 21st of November; on the following proposition as framed by the Senate : " The people desires the re-establishment of the Imperial dynasty in the person of Louis Napoleon Bonaparte, with the succession to his direct descendants, natural and legitimate, or adopted; and gives him the right to regulate the order of succession to the throne in the Bonaparte family."

It resulted that France demanded the restoration of the Bonaparte dynasty by a large majority.

Ayes 7,824,189
Noes 253,145
_____
Majority 7,571,044

On the 1st of December, the members of the Senate and of the Legislative Body repaired to Saint Cloud, to announce to the President of the Republic that he had been elected Emperor of France. The following sentences occur in the speech read by M. Billault, President of the Legislative Body, in presenting the report: "Your wish, Sire, is accomplishsd, a general, free, and secret ballot has been subjected to a strict examination before the eyes of all. Summing eight millions of votes, it gives to the legitimacy of your government the widest base on which any government in the world has ever been established. From one end of the country to the other, hastening to salute the man of their hopes and of their choice, our people have sufficiently proclaimed to the world that you are their Emperor, the Emperor elected by the people. Take then, Sire, from the hands of France, that illustrious crown which she offers to you : never has a royal brow worn one more legitimate or more popular."

On the next day, the 2nd of December, 1852, the Emperor quitted Saint Cloud about noon. He wore the full uniform of a General of Division, with the *grand cordon* of the Legion of Honour; and proceeded on horseback to the Palace of the Tuileries, the hereditary residence of the sovereigns of France. No notice had been given, nor preparation made for his official reception and the inauguration of the Empire. The people however thronged around him.

The *Moniteur* of the same date contained a proclamation of amnesty for all purely political offences ; on the sole condition of abstaining for the future from hostile acts against the existing Government : " The Emperor requires no more, and good sense as well as the exigencies of society can ask no less. The dearest wish of his majesty is to see effaced all traces of former divisions ; and retain of the past only the memory of services rendered. It shall not be the fault of the Prince who has been so lately crowned by the country, if any one of her children be longer severed from her." A general remission was at the same time granted of fines and other legal penalties : and all persons detained in the public prisons, excepting those charged with crimes of grave moral delinquency, were restored to liberty.

On the following morning (the 3rd) the Emperor visited the two chief Hospitals of Paris : the Hôtel-Dieu, and the Val-de-Grace. He went through all the wards of the sick, and spoke with kind interest to the patients ; and handed at parting, to the director of each establishment, a contribution to its funds of 10,000 francs.

It should not be omitted that, between his

visits to the two hospitals, the Emperor walked to the Cathedral of Notre-Dame, where, after a disuse of half a century, the noble hymn was again upraised,

"Domine, salvum fac Imperatorem."

CHAPTER VI.

Marriage of the Emperor (1853)—War in the Crimea—Birth
of the Prince Imperial (1856)—Providential Preservation
of the Emperor and Empress.

1853—1858.

THE close of the year 1852 had seen Louis
Napoleon raised to the Imperial dignity, amid
the general applause of the French people.

On the 22nd of January, 1853, the Emperor
convened the great bodies of the State: the
Senate, the Deputies, and the State-Council: at
the Palace of the Tuileries ; and, having taken his
seat on the throne, announced to them that he
had contracted a matrimonial engagement.

" I comply," said he, " with the wish so often
expressed by the nation, in coming to announce
to you my approaching marriage.

" The alliance which I form is not in accordance with the traditions of ancient policy. That
constitutes one of its advantages.

" France, by her successive revolutions, has
always separated herself abruptly from the rest of

Europe : it should be the object of every prudent Government to bring her back within the pale of the old monarchies. But this object is far more likely to be attained by a frank openness, and strict good faith in all transactions, than by those royal alliances which create a false sense of security, and substitute often the interests of a family for those of a nation. Besides, the examples of the past have implanted a belief,—a superstition, it may be,—in the mind of the people ; who cannot forget that, during the last seventy years, foreign princesses have ascended the throne but to see their race dispersed and proscribed by war or by revolution. One woman alone has seemed to bring prosperity, and to live above the rest in the memory of the people : and that woman, the good and unassuming wife of General Bonaparte, was not of blood royal.   *   *   *

" Thus impelled to depart from precedents hitherto followed, my marriage takes merely a private character. It remained only to make choice of the person. The object of my preference is of illustrious birth : French in heart, in education, and in the memory of blood shed by her father for the cause of the Empire, she possesses, as a Spaniard, the advantage of not having, in France, relations on whom it would be necessary to confer honours and dignities. Endued with every mental excellence, she will be the ornament of the throne, and, should the hour of danger arrive, one of its firmest supports. Catholic, and pious, she will address to Heaven the same prayers which I offer for the weal of France. Benevolent and good, she will, it is my firm trust, with the position, revive the virtues, of the Empress Josephine.

"I address myself therefore to France, and say: I have chosen a wife whom I love and respect rather than one unknown to me, whose espousal would have brought gain alloyed by sacrifices. Disdaining no other alliance, I follow in this the bent of my inclination, after consulting on it my reason and my judgment. In a word, by preferring independence of choice, the qualities of heart, and domestic happiness, to prejudices of dynasty and calculations of ambition, my state will be not less firm, it will be more free.

" I hope soon to present the Empress at Notre Dame to the people and to the army. The confidence which they repose in me assures their

K

sympathy towards the person of my choice. And you, gentlemen, on learning to know her, will acknowledge that, on this occasion also, I have been guided by Providence."

The civil marriage between "his Majesty Napoleon III., Emperor of the French, by the grace of God and the national will, and her Excellency Mademoiselle Eugénie de Montijo, Countess-Duchess of Téba, took place at the Palace of the Tuileries, on the 29th of January. On the following day the ecclesiastical ceremony was celebrated in the metropolitan church of Notre Dame.

The marriage of the Emperor has been, from the first, extremely popular among all orders of the community in France. Napoleon himself is not greeted with heartier acclamation than the lovely lady who shares his throne :

"A treasure-house of weal to France and him."*

In the Empress Eugénie, personal beauty and grace are heightened by the goodness and kindness expressed in every word and look, and still more in the thousand acts of charity which form

* "St. Clement's Eve."

the chief occupation and pleasure of her life. It may suffice to relate one act of the kind :—the city of Paris had voted a sum of 600,000 francs, intended for the purchase of a necklace, as a present to the bride of Napoleon III. on the celebration of their marriage. The Empress, in her acceptance of the gift, converted it into an offering for the foundation, in the French metropolis, of an Asylum for Female Orphans. The object of this institution is to assure to poor girls, bereaved of their parents, a provision for life by honest service, with an education suited to their condition, and not beyond it.

During the year 1853 the minds of men throughout Europe were kept in suspense and agitation through the aggressive conduct of Russia towards the Porte. The Czar Nicholas, indeed, so far from making any secret of his designs to seize the territory of the Sultan, proposed to England a share in the spoils of "the sick man," as the price of complicity in the transaction. The ideas of the Czar in reference to the affair are best conveyed in his own words, addressed to the British envoy at St. Petersburg (Sir H. G. Seymour) on the 11th of January,

к 2

1853 : "Tenez, nous avons sur les bras un homme malade,—un homme gravement malade,—ce sera, je vous le dis franchement, un grand malheur si, un de ces jours, il devait nous échapper, surtout avant que toutes les dispositions nécessaires fussent prises."

On a subsequent occasion (22nd February) the Emperor Nicholas explained more particularly his views as to the proposed division of the inheritance, "when the sick man died."—"The Principalities are," he said, "in fact an independent State, under my protection: this might so continue. Servia might receive the same form of government. So again with Bulgaria. As to Egypt, I quite understand the importance to England of that territory. I can then only say that, if, in the event of a distribution of the Ottoman succession, on the fall of the Empire, you should take possession of Egypt, I shall have no objection to offer. I would say the same of Candia: that island might suit you, and I do not know why it should not become an English possession."

The peculiar danger to the repose of Europe, arising from the ambitious projects of Russia, drew the serious attention of England and France.

In the words of M. Drouyn de l'Huys, to the French ambassador at Constantinople : " His Imperial Majesty's Government, in accordance with that of her Britannic Majesty, think the situation too menacing not to be narrowly watched." The united efforts of the two Western powers were energetically but vainly directed to turn the Russian Government from its purpose. A succession of menaces, together with the vast military and naval armaments which for months had been preparing on the very confines of Turkey, left no doubt as to the resolve of the Czar to resort to actual hostilities.

On the 2nd of July, an army under command of Prince Gortschakoff invaded Moldavia and Wallachia, provinces of the Ottoman Empire, under pretext of obtaining a "material guarantee" for satisfaction of any and all demands on the Porte. In thus occupying the Principalities, Russia violated both the territory of the Sultan and the special treaty signed by all the Great Powers of Europe, regarding that portion of his dominions. Nevertheless, Prince Gortschakoff, in a proclamation which he issued at the moment of his crossing the Pruth, the river-boundary between the Russian and Ottoman empires, claimed credit, on the part of his august master, for the virtue of magnanimity, in contenting himself, *provisionally*, with the Danubian provinces. " In his magnanimity, in his constant care to maintain peace in the East, as well as in Europe, the Emperor will avoid an aggressive war against Turkey, *as long as his dignity and the interests of his empire* will permit him to do so."

Threatening as the attitude of Russia had now become, the great Powers of Europe employed their joint influence to avert the effusion of blood. The French Emperor had from the first thrown the whole weight of his Government on the side of peace and public right ; and thus effected a closer union of purpose between the cabinets of England and France than ever before existed. Austria and Prussia were consequently drawn to associate themselves in the same spirit for the common cause. A thorough harmony prevailed between the four great Powers. Concurring entirely in their aim to dissuade Turkey from considering the invasion of her territory a case of war, they were at the same time no less unanimous in their determination to resist to the uttermost the unjust and violent pretensions of Russia.

Meantime the rod of Gortschakoff pressed heavily on Moldo-Wallachia. Not satisfied with levying forced contributions on its inhabitants, he compelled youths of the best families, on the plea of their disaffection to his yoke, to serve in the ranks of the Russian army. Notwithstanding, it was not till the 5th of October that the Porte published a formal declaration of war against the invader.

On the 31st of the same month, Count Nesselrode, Chancellor of the Russian Empire, in a diplomatic note addressed to its ministers at the Courts of Europe, wrote as follows : " We do not yet abandon the resolutions announced from the beginning, in our circular of the 2nd of July. At that period, his Majesty declared that, in temporarily occupying the Principalities, as a material guarantee, calculated to insure him the satisfaction which he demands, he did not wish to push further the measures of coercion, and would avoid an offensive war as long as his dignity and his interests would permit him. At the present time, and in spite of the new provocation which has now been addressed to him, the intentions of my august master remain the same."

An event occurred in the following month which took at once the question at issue out of the sphere of diplomacy, and removed all hope of its peaceful solution. On the 27th of November, the Russian Admiral Nachinoff, cruising in the Black Sea with two ships of the line and a brig, observed a Turkish squadron, consisting of seven frigates and some sloops, at anchor in the bay of Sinope, on the coast of Asia Minor ; and despatched the brig to convey the intelligence to Sebastopol. On receipt of the notice, four sail of the line, with several smaller vessels, left that port to reinforce the Russian Admiral. The effective strength of the two squadrons now stood as follows :

TURKISH.	RUSSIAN.
7 Frigates.	6 Ships of the line, of
2 Sloops.	which 3 were three-
1 Steamer.	deckers, carrying 120
	guns.
	2 Frigates.
	3 Steamers.

On the 30th, the Russians entered the harbour

of Sinope, with a favourable wind, and summoned the Turks to an immediate surrender. The Turks fought, however, with the courage of desperation, having no hope left of life, but determined to die with honour. The Russians kept up an incessant fire for three hours, and did not slacken it when their foe was incapable of further resistance. They turned their artillery also on the town of Sinope and its defenceless inhabitants, numbering from eight to ten thousand. The lives sacrificed were reckoned at 4,500. A steamer which had been despatched by signal from the Turkish Admiral, at the commencement of the attack, evaded several Russian vessels sent in pursuit of her, and carried the tidings to Constantinople. All the other vessels of the Turkish squadron were either sunk or set on fire. The Russians left the shores of the bay covered with the dead and the dying; the town a mass of half-burnt ruins, forsaken by all but those unable to fly; and retreated to their harbour of Sebastopol, glorying in the massacre of Sinope as if they had obtained a victory over some antagonist of equal strength.

The Czar, in an autograph letter to Prince

Mentschikoff, congratulated his navy on an achieve-
ment worthy of their flag : " The victory of Sinope
proves evidently that our Black Sea fleet has
shewn itself worthy of its destination. With
hearty joy I request you to communicate to my
brave seamen that I thank them for the success of
the Russian flag on behalf of the glory and honour
of Russia."

Very different was the manner in which the
affair was regarded by other nations. Lord
Clarendon, then Foreign Secretary, wrote to our
Minister at Saint Petersburg : " The feelings of
horror which this dreadful carnage could not but
create, have been general throughout all ranks and
classes of Her Majesty's subjects in this country."
" To prevent the recurrence of disasters such as
that of Sinope," Count Nesselrode was informed,
"the combined fleet will require, and, if necessary,
compel, Russian ships of war to return to Sebastopol, or the nearest port." The English and
French fleets, which, relying too credulously, as
the event proved, on the Czar's reiterated promise
that he would not pursue an offensive warfare
against Turkey, had remained at anchor in the
Bosphorus, entered now the Black Sea, and suf-

fered not a single Russian man-of-war to navigate its waters.

On the 29th of January, 1854, the Emperor Napoleon, as a last attempt at pacification, addressed the following letter to the Czar. It presents a concise summary of the causes which led to the campaign of the Crimea.

" To the Czar of Russia.
" Sire,

" The difference that has arisen between your Majesty and the Ottoman Porte has reached so serious a point that I feel it my duty to explain directly to your Majesty the part which France has taken in the question, and the measures which, according to my view, may yet avert the dangers that threaten the peace of Europe.

" The note which your Majesty has just addressed to my Government and to that of Queen Victoria tends to convey the impression that a system of pressure adopted from the first by the two maritime powers has alone envenomed the question at issue.

" That question, on the contrary, it seems to me, would still have remained one of treaty if the occupation of the Principalities had not at once removed it from the region of discussion to that of facts.

" Notwithstanding, your Majesty having once entered Wallachia, we still urged on the Porte not to consider such occupation a case of war, testifying thus our extreme desire for conciliation. In concert with England, Austria, and Prussia, I proposed to your Majesty a note, intended to give satisfaction to all parties. Your Majesty accepted it.

" But scarcely had this good news reached us when your minister, by explanatory comments, destroyed all its conciliatory effect, and prevented us thereby from pressing its implicit and absolute adoption at Constantinople. On the other side, the Porte had proposed certain modifications to the note, which the four Powers represented at Vienna considered to be unobjectionable : they did not meet the approval of your Majesty.

" Then it was that the Porte, wounded in its dignity, menaced in its independence, straitened through its efforts already made in raising an army to oppose that of your Majesty, declared war, as preferable to remaining in such a state of uncertainty and degradation. Our aid was invoked ;

we deemed the cause a just one ; the English and French squadrons received the order to anchor within the Bosphorus.

" Our attitude towards Turkey was protective but passive. We gave no encouragement to war. We poured incessantly into the ears of the Sultan counsels of peace and moderation, persuaded that such were the true means of arriving at an agreement ; and the four Powers concerted new propositions to be submitted to your Majesty.

" Your Majesty, meantime, with the calm which springs from the consciousness of strength, confined yourself to repelling, on the left bank of the Danube, and in Asia, the assaults of the Turks, and, with a moderation worthy the chief of a great empire, proclaimed your intention to remain on the defensive.

" Up to this point then, it is right to say, we were interested spectators, but spectators merely, of the contest, when the affair of Sinope came to compel us to a more decided part.

" France and England had not judged it expedient to land troops in aid of Turkey. Their flag, therefore, was not concerned in any conflict which took place on shore. But at sea it was widely different. Three thousand cannon were at the mouth of the Bosphorus, whose presence there spoke aloud to Turkey that the two principal maritime Powers would not permit her to be attacked by sea. The event of Sinope was as wounding to us as it was unexpected : for it is of little importance whether or not the Turks intended to pass munitions of war into Russian territory.

" In point of fact, Russian ships of the line attacked Turkish vessels of smaller size in Turkish waters, at anchor peacefully in a Turkish port: destroyed them in spite of the promise given to refrain from aggressive warfare, and in spite of the proximity of our squadrons. It was no longer our policy that received a blow, it was our martial honour. The cannon-shot fired at Sinope re-sounded sadly on the hearts of all who, in England and in France, felt keenly for the national dignity : all, with one accord, cried: "Wherever our cannon can reach, our allies should be respected."

" Hence came the order to our squadrons to enter the Black Sea, and to hinder, by force if needed, the recurrence of a similar disaster. Hence, too, the joint note sent to the Cabinet of Saint Petersburg, declaring that, if we prevented the Turks from waging an aggressive warfare on coasts belonging to Russia, we would protect them revictualling their forces on their own shores.

"With regard to our interdicting the navigation of the Black Sea to the Russian fleet, we put that upon a different condition: because it was of importance to us that, while the war lasted, we should hold a guarantee which might be equivalent to your occupation of the Turkish territory, and facilitate the conclusion of peace by affording the title of a desirable exchange.

" Such, Sire, are the facts of the case in their true order and sequence. It is clear that, having arrived at such a point, they must speedily bring on a definitive agreement or a decided rupture.

" Your Majesty has given so many proofs of your solicitude for the tranquillity of Europe; you have aided so powerfully, by your beneficial influence, in opposing the spirit of disorder; that I cannot doubt the resolution which you will take in the alternative that presents itself to your choice.

" If your Majesty desires a pacific result as much as I do, what more easy than to declare that an armistice shall immediately be signed, that affairs shall resume their diplomatic course, all hostility cease, all the belligerent forces retire from the positions taken up by them for warlike purposes ?

" Then would the Russian troops withdraw from the Principalities : our squadrons from the Black Sea. If your Majesty should prefer to treat directly with Turkey, you would nominate an ambassador, who would negotiate with a pleni-potentiary of the Sultan a convention to be submitted to a conference of the four Powers.

" Let your Majesty but adopt this plan, on which the Queen of England and I are perfectly in accord, tranquillity is re-established, and the world is satisfied. There is, in truth, nothing in this proposal that is unworthy of your Majesty, nothing which can wound your honour. But if, from a motive difficult to comprehend, your Majesty should return a refusal, then France as well as England would be obliged to leave to the arbitrement of arms and the chances of war that which might be decided at once by reason and justice.

" Let not your Majesty suppose that the slightest animosity prevails in my heart : it experiences no other sentiments than those expressed by your Majesty in your letter of the 17th of January, 1853, wherein you wrote to me : 'Our relations ought to be sincerely amicable, based on the same intentions : the maintenance of order, love of peace, respect to treaties, and mutual good-will.'* This programme is worthy of the sovereign who traced it, and I do not hesitate to say that I, on my part, have remained faithful to it.

" I pray your Majesty to believe in the sincerity of the sentiments which I profess, and with which I am,

" Sire,

" Your good friend,

" NAPOLEON.

" January 29, 1854."

To this letter, so conciliatory in its tenor, the Czar returned a positive refusal to accede to the proposed arrangement. All means of persuasion having been exhausted, France and England, acting in concert, declared war against Russia on

* " Nos rélations doivent être sincèrement amicales, reposer sur les mêmes intentions : maintien de l'ordre, amour de la paix, respect aux traités, et bienveillance réciproque."

the same day, March 27th, 1854. Thus, after a state of peace which had lasted for forty years between the great European powers, the first note of conflict was sounded. The result, it is well known, was to prove, after a struggle of unexampled fierceness, that France and England possessed strength to repel and chastise the insatiable ambition of the Czar, aiming at the seizure of Constantinople as a sure step to supremacy in Europe. The success of the allied powers was not, however, achieved until the best blood of both nations had been poured out like water, and mourning brought to hearths and homes of every rank and class throughout our land.

Louis Napoleon declared more than once his resolve to proceed to the seat of war in the East, and put himself at the head of his troops before Sebastopol; but political exigencies over-ruled this intention of engaging personally in the campaign. It was at a later period, in the war undertaken by France for the defence of Sardinia, in 1859, that the Emperor gave the world ample opportunity to judge of his capacity as a military commander.

While on the topic of the war in the Crimea of

1854-55, it is curious to recall the fact that, full
a thousand years before, the Russians were absolute masters of the Black Sea ; a nation of pirates
on a large scale. Having commenced their
existence as a nation at Novogorod, and extended
their frontier to the Baltic on the west, and as
far south as Kiow (or Kieff,) they made their
first attempt, in two hundred large canoes, to
pillage Constantinople in the year 865. The
alarm of the Greek Emperor, Michael III. was
excessive, and relieved only by a providential
storm, which scattered the unseaworthy flotilla of
his assailants. Levesque, the historian of Russia,
furnishes some details respecting this expedition.
The Emperor Michael had quitted his capital with
an armed force, to make war on some Arab enemies.
" Il reçoit un courier du gouverneur de Constantinople, qui lui apprend que les Russes approchent
sur deux cents vaisseaux, et que la ville est
menacée. L'Empereur retourne sur ses pas avec
son armée, mais quelque diligence qu'il puisse
faire, il trouve que les Russes ont déjà ravagé les
bords de la mer noire, que les rives du bosphore
de Thrace ont été livrées au feu et à la flamme,
et que la flotte ennemie ferme l'entrée de Con-

L 2

stantinople.   Ce ne fut qu'avec des difficultés
extrêmes qu'il parvint à se jeter dans la ville.
. . . Heureusement une tempête disperse la flotte
ennemie ; Oskhold, le chef de cette expédition,
demande en même temps la paix et le baptême, et
retourne à Kief."*

Thus, at the very epoch when the Danes and
other pirates of the North Sea were ravaging the
coasts of Britain, the Russians, after a similar
fashion, were wasting with fire and sword the
shores of the Euxine.   Towards the close of the
fourteenth century, the Mogul conquerors overspread those regions, and seemed to have blotted
out the Russian name.   But on the collapse of
the Mogul empire in Europe, the Russian power,
which had been kept down but not extinguished,
sprang up into fresh life in its first cradle, Novogorod, and has since, as we know too well,
advanced its fortresses into the heart of Europe,
destroyed the kingdom of Poland, and depressed
its other neighbours, Sweden and Denmark.

The enormous expenditure attendant on a
campaign such as that undertaken by France and
England against the common foe, though a minor

* *Histoire de Russie*, vol. i. p. 75.

item in the amount of human suffering, the tears, and the bloodshed, which are the cost of war, forms yet no insignificant portion of its penalties. To meet the occasion, Louis Napoleon adopted a mode which had no precedent in the history of financial policy, the success of which exceeded the most sanguine expectation. Instead of em- ploying, as usual in such cases, the agency of capitalists and contractors for a national loan, the Emperor made his appeal directly to the people, who responded to the call by bringing willingly far more than he required. The first amount asked was five hundred million francs : the people brought more than four times that amount. Later, the Government asked a supple- mentary loan of three hundred million francs, or twelve millions sterling : the people brought nearly five thousand million francs, or two hundred millions sterling.*

* Even the above proportions have been greatly exceeded since. In the month of August, 1868, an official circular from the Minister of Finance conveyed some details to the subscribers to a loan just then effected. The summary is given in an article in *The Times* of the 25th of that month : " The amount of money required by the French Minister of Finance was rather more than eighteen millions sterling. Instead of eighteen millions sterling, it became more than

Amid the war that raged in the Crimea, the arts of peaceful industry were still remembered by nations thus engaged in deadly strife. The Great Exhibition at Paris, in the Spring of 1855, gathered together at one view the various works of human skill and the national products of different climes from all quarters of the globe. The speech made by the Emperor of the French at the close of the Exhibition, to an auditory of sixty thousand persons, advocated strongly the restoration of peace. " The Exhibition now about to close offers to the world a great spectacle. It is during a war of serious character that, from all points of the globe, persons the most distinguished in science, arts, and industry, have come to Paris to exhibit the result of their toils. This assemblage, under such circumstances, is due, I rejoice to believe, to the general conviction that the war in which we are engaged is menacing to those only who provoked it ; that it has been carried on in the interest of all, and that Europe sees in it no prognostic of peril, but rather a guarantee of security and independence.

six hundred millions sterling ; thirty-four times as much as was required."

"Nevertheless, in view of the many wonders displayed before our eyes, the first impression produced is a desire for peace. Peace alone, in fact, can develope still farther these remarkable fruits of the human intelligence. You will naturally wish with me, that such a peace may be prompt and durable. But that it may be durable, it is necessary that it resolve distinctly the question for which the war was undertaken. That it may be prompt, it is indispensable that Europe declare herself for one side or for the other; since, without the pressure of public opinion, the contest between the great powers threatens to be prolonged; whereas, on the contrary, if Europe decide to pronounce who is right or who is wrong, it will be a great step towards the desired solution. At the present epoch of civilization, the successes of armies, however brilliant, are but passing triumphs; it is always public opinion which obtains the final victory."

After the close of the Exhibition, the Emperor, in an address to the French Legislature, alluded in the following terms to the visit of Queen Victoria to Paris : "The Queen of Great Britain, wishing to confer on our country a mark of her confidence and esteem, and to render our relations more intimate, has visited France. The enthusiastic welcome which she received must have proved to her how deep were the sentiments that her presence inspired, and how calculated to fortify the alliance between the two nations."

The Empress Eugénie, on the 16th of March, 1856, gave birth to a son. The heir to the Imperial throne of France, received the baptismal names, Napoléon Louis Eugène.

On the 14th of January, 1858, an attempt at assassination, as foul and dastardly as any recorded in the annals of crime, occurred in the streets of Paris. The chief conspirator, an Italian named Orsini, had hired three other Italians, ruffians of lower grade than himself, to join him in carrying out his project. They were provided each with a shell charged with fulminating powder; and took their stand, on the eve of the 14th, at the door of the Opera, between eight and nine o'clock, the hour at which it was known that the Emperor and Empress of the French were expected to visit the theatre. Suspicions had arisen in the minds of the police, and one of the assassins was arrested at the private entrance of the building just a quarter of an hour before the arrival of their Majesties. Scarcely had their carriage reached the spot when three shells thrown under it, in rapid succession, burst, with a terrific noise and stifling smoke, into a tempest of iron fragments, dealing wounds and death among the hundreds assembled around. General Roquet, an aide-de-camp of the Emperor, was wounded severely, within the carriage, by the explosion, and countless injuries were inflicted on attendants and by-standers. In the midst of the scene of confusion and terror, the Emperor and Empress maintained a calm self-possession worthy of them. They inquired into the extent of the mischief done, from which they had been so marvellously protected, and into the cases and condition of the sufferers; and then entered the theatre for a while, to assure the public by their presence of their providential preservation and safety. On the morrow they visited the wounded in the hospitals, and traversed the Boulevards of the city without any escort, greeted everywhere by the warmest acclamations.

Orsini, the chief of the assassins, struck by one of his own projectiles, was tracked by the blood falling from his wound, to a café, and there arrested.*

On the 17th of January, at the opening of the Legislative Chambers, the Emperor, in his speech to them, referred to the recent outrage : " I cannot conclude without speaking to you of the late criminal attempt, and rendering thanks to heaven for the protection so visibly afforded to the Empress and me. I lament that so many victims should have been sacrificed in order to assail a single life. Such conspiracies bring with them, however, more than one useful lesson. 1. The faction which resorts to means so desperate proves thereby its own weakness and impotence. 2. Never has an assassination, even if successful in its immediate object, advantaged those who armed the hand of the assassin. Neither the blow which struck Cæsar, nor that which slew Henry IV. profited the authors of those murders. God permits sometimes the just to fall, but He never suffers the cause of the assassin to triumph. Thus, such attempts can shake neither my confidence in the present nor my faith in the future :

---

* He was executed with one of his accomplices ; two were sentenced to penal servitude for life.

if I live, the Empire lives on with me; and should I fall, the Empire would survive, and be strengthened even by my death, since the indignation of the people and of the army would be a fresh support to the throne of my son.

" Let us then face the future with confidence ; and, without disquieting apprehensions, apply ourselves to our wonted labours for the welfare and greatness of the country. *Dieu protège la France.*"

CHAPTER VII.

THE CAMPAIGN OF ITALY.

1859.

A GREAT demonstration of public feeling took place on the departure of the Emperor Napoleon III. for the Italian Campaign. "It was at five o'clock," an eye-witness* relates, " on a summer evening (May 10, 1859) that the Emperor quitted the Tuileries, after having attended with his household a religious service in the chapel of the palace. He was in an open carriage, in military undress, and accompanied solely by the Empress; his brilliant staff having preceded him to the 'Gare de Lyon,' the Paris railway station for Marseilles. The people, who had long waited impatiently for his appearance, filled the streets, windows, balconies, and even house-tops. His carriage proceeded at a walking pace, often brought to a stand-still by the crowd. It was no longer a

* M. Mullois.

shout, but a thunder of acclamation, with stamping of feet, clapping of hands, waving of hats. Many a hearty grasp of the hand was exchanged between the Emperor and those of the throng who succeeded in forcing their way to the first rank. Even the women and children took part in the demonstration, and threw garlands of flowers into the carriage with cries of : *Que Dieu vous protège!* The Emperor rose frequently from his seat to acknowledge these hearty farewells, and was visibly affected, though his countenance retained its habitual calm expression. The Empress at his side could not restrain her tears, while, from time to time, with her gracious manner and sweet smile, she thanked the people for their outburst of loyal affection. If any diversity of opinion existed elsewhere on the policy of the Italian campaign, it seemed certain that between sovereign and people there was but one heart and one mind on the subject. ' Sire,' exclaimed a workman, ' if you want soldiers, you have but to speak the word, we are all ready.' "

The causes which made the war of Italy a national necessity for Sardinia and France, even after their assent to the conditions proposed by a

Congress of the great powers for preserving the peace of Europe, are explained in a letter from Count Cavour to Count Buol, and in a proclamation from the Emperor Napoleon to the French people.

LETTER from Count Cavour, Sardinian Minister for Foreign Affairs, to Count Buol, Chief Minister of Austria.

"Turin, April 26, 1859.

" Monsieur le Comte,

" Baron Kellersberg placed in my hands on the 23rd inst., at half-past six in the evening, the letter which your Excellency has done me the honour to address to me, dated the 19th of this month, in the name of the Imperial Government, requiring me to reply, by a simple ' Yes ' or ' No,' to the invitation conveyed to us to reduce our army to a peace footing, and to disband the bodies of troops formed of Italian volunteers : adding that if at the expiration of three days your Excellency should have received no reply, or if the reply received should not be satisfactory, his Majesty the Emperor of Austria has determined to resort to arms, in order to impose by force those measures which form the object of his communication.

" The question of the disarmament of Sardinia, which constitutes the base of the demand made by your Excellency, has been the subject of numerous negotiations between the great powers and the Government of his Majesty. These negotiations have resulted in a proposition drawn up by England, to which France, Prussia, and Russia, have given assent. Sardinia has accepted it without reserve or qualification.

" As your Excellency cannot be ignorant either of the proposition made or of Sardinia's reply to it, I can add nothing to your knowledge of the dispositions of the King's Government relative to the difficulties which hindered the re-assembling of the Congress.

" The conduct of Sardinia in this conjuncture has been appreciated by Europe. Whatever may be the consequences resulting from it, the King, my august master, is convinced that the responsibility of them will recoil on those who were the first to arm ; who have rejected the proposition drawn up by one of the great powers, and recognised as just and reasonable by the others ; and

who now substitute for it a threatening summons.

> " I avail myself of this occasion, &c.,
>
> " C. CAVOUR."

" To the French People.

> " Palace of the Tuileries.
> " 3 May, 1859."

" Frenchmen,

" Austria, by invading the territory of our
ally the King of Sardinia, declares war against us ;
setting at nought treaties and justice, and menacing
our frontiers.   All the great powers have protested
against this aggression.

" Since Piedmont has accepted every condition
proposed for the preservation of peace, we may
naturally ask, what inducement can have led to
this sudden invasion ?   It is simply this :—
Austria has pushed matters to such an extremity
that either her dominion must extend to the Alps,
or Italy must be free to the Adriatic.   The
smallest portion of that country which retains its
independence is a peril to her sway.

" Hitherto, moderation has been the guide of
my conduct : energy becomes now my chief duty.

" Let France arm, and say resolutely to
Europe : ' I wish for no foreign conquest, but I
desire to maintain firmly my national policy : I
observe the faith of treaties towards others, provided they be not violated against myself : I respect
the territory and the rights of neutral powers, but
avow openly my sympathy for a people whose
history blends itself with my own, and who groan
beneath the yoke of the stranger.'

" France has testified her abhorrence of anarchy.
Her will has bestowed on me a power sufficiently
strong to reduce to impotence the promoters of
disorder, and the incorrigible partisans of effete
factions, whom we see in continual correspondence
with our enemies. But France has not therefore
renounced her part in the work of civilization.
Her natural allies have ever been found in the
ranks of those who seek the amelioration of mankind, and when France draws the sword it is not
to enslave, but to enfranchise.

" The object, then, of this war is not to give
Italy a change of masters, but to restore her to
herself, and thus we shall have on our frontiers a
friendly power, indebted to us for independence.

" We go to that classic land, ennobled to us by

M

so many victories, to retrace there the footsteps of our fathers. May we but prove ourselves worthy of them.

" I go shortly to place myself at the head of the army. I leave in France the Empress and my son. Aided by the counsels and experience of the Emperor's last surviving brother,* she will shew herself equal to the greatness of her mission. I confide them to the valour of that army which will remain in France for the safety of our frontiers and the protection of the domestic hearth : I confide them to the loyalty of the National Guard ; to the entire nation ; who will surround them with that affection and devotion of which I receive daily so many proofs.

" Courage, then, and concord ! The world shall see yet again that our country has not degenerated. Providence will bless our efforts, for the cause must be holy in the sight of Heaven, which rests on justice, humanity, love of country and of independence.

" NAPOLEON."

The train appointed to carry the Emperor and his suite left Paris at a quarter after six ; the

---

* Prince Jerome.

Empress accompanying him as far as to Montereau, about twenty leagues from the capital.
From Montereau the train proceeded with scarcely
a halt, and reached Marseilles about noon on the
day following.   The Emperor went from the
station direct to the port, and embarked at once on
board the Imperial yacht *La Reine Hortense*, which
waited to convey him to the army of Italy.
About 2 o'clock, p.m., the vessel was clear of the
harbour, and soon after noon next day (12 May)
entered the port of Genoa.

The scene witnessed there, on the arrival of *La
Reine Hortense*, is described as a spectacle rarely
parallelled.   Eight hundred vessels of various
nations lay at anchor, and among them English,
French, Sardinian men-of-war, with yards manned,
and dressed in flags.   English " *Hurrahs !* "
mingled with the shouts of " *Evviva la Francia !* "
" *Evviva Napoleone !* "   The spacious and beautiful
harbour was covered with boats, each one bringing
its freight of flower-wreaths.   " Les fleurs
pleuvaient :" it was said : nosegays were showered
in such profusion as to form a flying arch over the
boat which conveyed the Emperor to the landing-
place ; while, the weather being perfectly calm,

M 2

all brilliant colours of flowers and flags were reflected in the still clear waters, as in a mirror. One thing was particularly noticed in the rejoicings at the landing of Napoleon III. in Italy : not a shade of doubt mingled with the universal exultation. The same confidence appeared in all ranks, that the union of the Italian and French arms would achieve results as triumphant as, in the event, they proved to be.

The Emperor was received on shore by the Prince of Carignano ; Count Cavour, President of the Council ; Regnaud de Saint-Jean d'Angély, Commander-in-chief of the Imperial Guard ; and by them conducted to the Palazzo Reale, where, at an early hour on the following morning, King Victor Emmanuel arrived to welcome his potent ally. Most of that day was given to conferences with the Commissaries-General, in regard to arrangements to be adopted for the subsistence of the troops during the approaching operations in the field.

On the morrow, 14 May, the Emperor proceeded to join the main body of his army at Alessandria, the principal stronghold of Piedmont, and its central depôt for provisions and munitions of war.

Four French corps-d'armée were now assembled
around this fortress : the 1st and 2nd, under com-
mand of Marshal Baraguey d' Hilliers and General
Mac-Mahon, had come by sea, from Marseilles and
Toulon to Genoa :   the 3rd and 4th, under Marshal
Canrobert and General Niel, had entered Piedmont
through the passes of the Alps.   The 5th corps,
commanded by Prince Napoleon, remained at
Genoa.   The above five corps-d'armée, with the
Imperial Guard, numbered about 125,000 men.
The Sardinian army, about 55,000, raised the
total of the allied forces to 180,000.

The Emperor fixed his head-quarters at Alessandria as his base of operations, till enabled to
decide on the final dispositions for a movement in
advance :   and proceeded immediately to a study
of the surrounding country, visiting assiduously
every point of importance.   In order to follow the
plan of strategy on which he resolved, it is indispensable to take a view of the position occupied by
the Austrian forces on his arrival in Italy.   They
had begun to cross the river Ticino, the barrier
that separates Lombardy and Piedmont, on the
26th of April, and, though their movements were
not rapid, accomplished in a few days, without

meeting impediment, the transport of five Austrian corps-d'armée into Sardinian territory. Considerable vacillation seems to have prevailed in their subsequent councils, since, instead of pushing forward to attain any definite object, they wasted time in "marchings and counter-marchings." It is probable that their first intention was an advance on Turin ; but that the arrival of French troops at Alessandria, exposing the Austrians to the danger of a flank attack on their road to the capital of Sardinia, induced them to change their plans, and retrace their steps towards the Ticino. By their slowness and indecision they deprived themselves of any advantage which might have arisen from being earliest in the field and striking the first blow. On the other hand, no time was lost by the Emperor in affording Sardinia the moral support of an allied power marching to her succour. On the 30th of April, the head of Canrobert's columns entered Turin. Shortly afterwards the French legions were concentrated round Alessandria in sufficient force to make a stand against all assailants.

At the middle of May, the right extremity of the line held by the allied armies was formed by the

1st division of the 1st corps-d'armée, under command of General Forey. It was stationed near to
the village of Montebello, a field already celebrated
in the military annals of France, being the same
on which, sixty years before, (9 June, 1800),
Lannes won his title of Duke of Montebello, by a
victory over the Austrians. About five miles
beyond, is another village, Casteggio,* in rear of
which a strong Austrian detachment was posted ;
and, as the hostile forces were daily extending
themselves towards each other in that direction,
it was evident that a collision at some point must
speedily ensue. On the 20th of May, about noon,
a large body of Austrians advanced upon Casteggio,
and took possession of the village in overwhelming
force, after a valiant defence by some Sardinian
cavalry stationed there. The Sardinians fell back
in good order on Montebello, which they likewise
defended for a considerable time, till, yielding to
superior numbers, they retreated on the French
division. General Forey, who on the first alarm
supposed it to be a mere *reconnaissance*, or exploring party, soon discovered, beyond a doubt, that

* Once a Roman military station of importance, reduced
to ashes by Hannibal.

the offensive movement was of a serious character, finding himself in presence of two strong hostile columns advancing on his outposts. These posts had been recently strengthened by order of the Emperor, in anticipation of such an attack. It partook nevertheless, in some degree, the nature of a surprise. Forey, collecting hastily a few battalions and a battery of artillery, made every possible effort, seconded vigorously by charges from the Piedmontese cavalry, to hold his antago- nists in check until reinforcements could arrive from his division. A short time brought up other French troops, and the conflict now raged in that close hand-to-hand fighting by which, as military authorities agree, after all that manœuvring can do, the fate of battles is usually decided. The furious and repeated rushes of the French pre- vailed over the obstinate valour of their opponents : the Austrians, notwithstanding their superiority of numbers, gave way. Every step, however, was marked by carnage and destruction. The crops of rye and other grain, which at that time grew high in the fields, concealed bands of Tyrolese marksmen and skirmishers ; who, as the advance of the French trampled under foot the corn, rose to sight, seeming to realise the old fable of armed men springing out of the earth. The Austrians, finally, were repelled to the village of Montebello where they renewed the combat still more fiercely. Every window poured its volleys ; every house was turned into a fortress ; they were carried, one by one, frequently not until the last defender had fallen. At length, the Austrians were driven from the village, but at its further extremity entrenched themselves for a final stand at a cemetery, planting cannon on a rising-ground, to command the road. Here ensued the most sanguinary struggle of the day. Forey, gathering his troops from all the streets and lanes of the place, poured them in an irresistible flood over the low walls of the cemetery, and carried this last position at the point of the bayonet, with shouts of " Vive l' Empereur ! " The Austrians retreated in disorder to Casteggio, which they evacuated soon afterwards. The combat had lasted from noon till half-past six.

At six o'clock on the following morning, (the 21st) the Emperor left Alessandria, accompanied by Generals Forey and Martimprey ; Larrey, the Surgeon-in-chief ; the Abbé Laine, and another chaplain ; to visit the field of Montebello, and bring help and sympathy to the wounded. A French writer* tells us : " Il trouva chacun à son poste, aumôniers et chirurgiens, ceux-ci parlant à l'âme des mourants, ceux-là cherchant à ramener la vie parmi les victimes que le combat avait frappé. . . . C'était un spectacle touchant de voir ces malheureux se soulever sur leur lit de souffrance, et oublier de douloureuses blessures pour acclamer leur Empereur."

It appears that a large proportion of the Austrian force engaged in the combat of Montebello were young recruits ill qualified to cope with the French veterans—*les vieux d'Afrique.* " Of about 200 prisoners captured by the French," one present on the occasion reports, " there were scarcely a dozen who had reached the age of twenty-five ; many were mere boys ; one, the son of an Austrian count, had entered the service only twenty days before, and seemed little pleased with his *début.* The field of battle was strewn with dead, mown down by rows. The corn-crops, which on the previous day had been standing full and ripening for the harvest, on the morning

* M. de Bazancourt.

after the combat were crushed and trodden down, covered with gory flakes, dried and blackened in the sun. Caps, collars, vests, pieces of cloth, stained with blood, lay on every side. I stumbled on two bodies which had been quite hid under long grass ; one, a lad of about fifteen years ; he wore suspended by a ribbon round his neck the miniature of an aged female, probably of his mother." " I had the fortune," another writer relates, " to lay hands on a stripling who fought like a young tiger : I knocked up a musket that was levelled at him, and seized him by the collar, to prevent further unpleasant consequences. ' Yield, boy :' I cried ; whereon he handed me his sword, but, though I saved his life, he would not thank me for it."

The success of Montebello, flattering to the military prowess of the French, afforded them no sufficient encouragement to a direct attack on the main body of the Austrians. Count Gyulai, their Commander-in-Chief, having received reinforcements which raised his numbers to about 200,000 men, held a position at the close of the month of May, in the angle formed by the confluence of the Ticino with the Po near to the town of Pavia, which presented almost insuperable obstacles to an assailant. The Emperor resolved therefore, instead of attacking, to turn it.

In order to conceal his design, he massed French and Sardinian troops on his right, under command of King Victor Emmanuel, to make a demonstration against the Austrian encampments. At the same time, the Emperor prepared to carry his army by the left towards Novara. Two severe combats which ensued, on the 30th and 31st May, at Palestro, resulting in favour of the allies, tended to confirm the impression that their chief efforts were directed to that quarter. Meanwhile, the main army of the French, by sudden and rapid marches, had reached Novara, and taken up there the same ground on which King Charles Albert had battled, ten years before (23 March, 1849,) for the freedom of Italy.

The town of Novara is about fifty miles E.N.E. from Tunis; on the high road, which, leading from that capital to Milan, crosses the Ticino by the bridge of Buffalora, and passes through Magenta, a village two miles on the left or Lombard side of the river. The object of the strategic movement so ably planned and boldly executed by the Emperor was to secure the passage of the Ticino for his army, concentrate it at Magenta, and advance upon Milan.

By his direction, on the 2nd June, the *voltigeurs*, or light division, of the Guard, under command of General Camon, accompanied by a battery of artillery and a squadron of cavalry, proceeded to throw three pontoon bridges across the Ticino, opposite to Turbigo, a village of Lombardy situate about seven miles above Buffalora. This work was accomplished without difficulty, and was intended for the passage of the 2nd corps d'armeé (Mac-Mahon) the next day.

On the 3rd, accordingly, that corps advanced from Novara, and crossing the Ticino on the same afternoon, established itself firmly at Turbigo. The Emperor, who was present to witness the success of the movement, and the repulse of an Austrian column which had come from Milan to oppose the progress of the French, returned at 5 p.m. to Novara.

Our narrative brings us now to the 4th of June, the day on which the great contest was to be decided, its stake being the domination of the Austrians in Lombardy. On the morning of that

memorable day, the Emperor, having under his
immediate command the Grenadier division of the
Imperial Guard, about 5,000 in number, with five
batteries of artillery and two squadrons of light-
horse, crossed the bridge of Buffalora, occupying
thus the centre of approaching operations ; the
point, that is, at which battle was first joined and
towards which all its lines converged. The 3rd
and 4th corps d'armée (Canrobert and Niel)
received orders to follow in support of the Guard,
and to pass the river at the same point. The
corps of Mac-Mahon was to march at the same
time from Turbigo on Buffalora and Magenta.
Difficulties, however, arising chiefly from the bad
state of the roads, delayed the execution of these
combinations ; and Canrobert and Niel were unable
to reach the scene of action until the evening of
the day. When the Grenadiers crossed the bridge
with much precaution, towards the hour of noon,
it was impossible for them to foretell what amount
of resistance they might have to encounter on
their further advance : all was calm and still
around, and nothing indicated the vicinity of a
foe. The country before them presented a view
of corn-fields and vineyards, interspersed with

groves of mulberry and other trees ; a fair and peaceful scene, soon to be shaken by the cries of war, the tramp of battalions, and the roar of artillery. For, on the crests of some neighbour- ing heights, Austrian troops began to appear from time to time, and the movements which took place among them at various points seemed to shew that they were in considerable force. Distant interchange of shots ensued between the skir- mishers on either side, and the Emperor remained anxiously waiting some sign of the approach of Mac-Mahon.

That General had left Turbigo at 10 a.m., in two columns : the first, headed by himself, directed on the right to Buffalora, which he calculated on reaching in two hours and half : the second, under General Espinasse, by a different route to Magenta. About one o'clock, a sharp fire of musketry, followed by a rapid dis- charge of cannon, was heard near the village of Buffalora. General Mac-Mahon was arriving there. The Emperor ordered an immediate advance in that direction. Two brigades of the Guard, commanded by Generals Cler and Wimpffen, rushed impetuously forward, and carried several formidable positions occupied by the enemy. The further progress of the French was however arrested by the continually increasing number of their opponents. Austrian bayonets glittered on all sides, threatening to overwhelm the Emperor's comparatively small band; and it was only by the most determined efforts that he could stand his ground and maintain command of the bridge. At this crisis, the cannon of Mac-Mahon suddenly ceased.

In order to throw light on events at this time in progress, it is necessary to recur to the operations of the Austrian army under Count Gyulai. He had become aware, on the night of the 2nd of June, of the manœuvres of the French, and, re-crossing the Ticino near to Pavia, in all haste pushed forward by forced marches towards Magenta. They were part of his troops which now attacked the French at the bridge : but his main army was directed to occupy Magenta. Mac-Mahon, as he drew near to Buffalora, perceived that he had in front of him the Austrians in very superior force. Their heavy masses covered the country between Buffalora and Magenta; and came on with manifest intention of interposing betwixt the two columns of the French corps, and thus cutting off the division of Espinasse from the rest of the army. Mac-Mahon suspended, in consequence, his forward movement, in order to give time for the junction of his two columns ; and this explains the cessation of firing already mentioned. An officer of his staff was dispatched to General Espinasse, who promised to operate the proposed junction within an hour. But he had difficulties of his own to contend against, finding also the enemy on his path. The hour elapsed, and Mac-Mahon, intolerant of prolonged suspense, accompanied by a few officers of his staff and a platoon of light horse, by a sudden impulse, galloped off across country at full speed. They dashed over hedges and ditches, through thickets where the horses had to breast their way by sheer force. In mid course they burst upon a party of Tyrolese skirmishers, ambushed in some corn. The marksmen, amazed at the irruption of wild horsemen, instead of using their rifles, held them up with their bonnets on the muzzles, in token of surrender. The riders, without paying them the least regard, pursued their headlong race ; and, a little further on, were charged by a small detachment of *uhlans*, (lancers) whom they encountered by drawing the sabre, but not the rein, never slackening speed nor deviating from their course for a single instant, until they reached General Espinasse. A few words sufficed between the two Generals, to give and receive the necessary instructions. The last direction of Mac-Mahon, as he turned to gallop back to his division, was " *Hâtez vous*, surtout."

Meanwhile, the state of affairs at the bridge was becoming more and more critical. Regnaud de Saint-Jean-d'Angély, and the Grenadiers of the Guard, fighting under the eye of the Emperor, displayed the utmost energy and resolution, but were nearly exhausted in the struggle against numbers. It was four o'clock, and the corps d'armée of Marshal Canrobert had not yet appeared. But the cannon of Mac-Mahon began now to thunder again. His columns had completed their junction, and, presenting a compact front, were marching anew upon Magenta. The Austrian army opposed the most strenuous resistance to their advance. The nature of the country, wooded and laid out in vineyards, being

unfavourable to the use of artillery, and prevent-
ing the formation of a regular line of battle, the
contest was carried on in a succession of deadly
encounters with the rifle and the bayonet. An
eye-witness* writes to an English journal : " The
frightful scene of carnage on all the ground,
which the Austrians defended inch by inch but
had to leave at last, is like the remains of a
great rag-fair : shakoes, knapsacks, muskets,
shoes, cloaks, tunics, linen, all stained with blood,
and speaking of the obstinate resistance even now
when the greater part of the wounded have been
removed and the dead mostly buried. Of how
many dramas of heroism and ferocity, of how
many tragedies of woes and misery, must this
have been the scene ! " — Finally, the French
succeeded in pressing back the Austrians along
their whole line, and in cutting their way with
the bayonet to the village of Magenta, which both
sides felt to be the key of the position. Here
the conflict raged with redoubled fury in the close
narrow streets ; the cries and shouts of the com-
batants mingling with the rattle of musketry and
the roar of cannon. At length the Austrians

* Correspondent of *The Times*.

were driven out of the place, leaving 6,000 prisoners and four pieces of artillery in the hands of the victors.

The corps of Canrobert and Niel had by this time joined the Emperor, and the fate of the day could no longer be doubted. Their opponents, beaten back at all points, were in full and hasty retreat, leaving the French, at eight o'clock, undisputed masters of the field.

The Battle of Magenta cannot be classed in the number of sterile victories. Its immediate effect was to free Piedmont from her invaders, and to open to the conquerors the gates of Milan. On the morning of the 8th of June, the Emperor of the French and the King of Sardinia made their entry together into the capital of Lombardy. At half-past seven a.m., the sovereigns, with their staffs, met at the Vercellina gate, in front of the triumphal arch, " *Arco della Pace*," which forms the entrance to the fine military square, *Piazza d'Armi*. Here Marshal Regnaud de Saint-Jean d'Angély, with the Imperial Guard drawn up in line of battle, awaited their arrival. Great preparations had been made by the inhabitants of the city to give a worthy reception to the liberators of Lombardy. But they had not been expected before eleven in the forenoon; and the houses whose roofs and balconies displayed the united banners of France and Sardinia were still closed at the early hour when Napoleon III. and Victor Emmanuel, attended by a single squadron of the Guard, rode into Milan. The following proclamation was published on the same day.

" Italians !

" The fortune of war having brought me into the capital of Lombardy, it remains for me to inform you why I am here.

" When Austria unjustly attacked Piedmont, I resolved to support my ally the King of Sardinia. The honour and interests of France imposed this duty on me. Your enemies, who are mine also, have endeavoured to diminish the universal sympathy with which Europe regards your cause, by representing that I make war from personal ambition, or to extend the territory of France. If there are persons who so misunderstand their epoch, I am not of the number. In the present enlightened state of public opinion, greatness is to be achieved far more by moral influence than by barren victories : and it is that moral influence

at which I aim, in contributing, with pride, to
render free one of the finest countries in Europe.

"The welcome which you have already accorded
me is a sufficient proof that you have not mis-
construed my motives. I come with no precon-
certed plan to displace other sovereigns, or to
establish my own authority: my army will have
but two occupations; to combat your enemies, and
to aid in the maintenance of internal order; it will
offer no impediment to the free and just development of your wishes. The favour of Providence
opens sometimes before nations, as before indi-
viduals, a way of rising suddenly to greatness,
but only on condition that they know how to
profit by such opportunity. Take advantage of
that which presents itself to you. Your desire
for independence, so long expressed, so often
deceived, will now be fulfilled, if you shew yourselves worthy of it. Unite your efforts in one
sole aim, the emancipation of your country.
Range yourselves under military organisation.
Haste to join the banner of the King Victor
Emmanuel, whose example has already so nobly
guided you on the path to honour. Remember
that, without discipline, there is no army; and,

animated by the sacred fire of patriotism, be
soldiers,—only soldiers,—to day: to-morrow you
will be free citizens of a great nation.

"Napoleon.
"Imperial Head-Quarters,
"Milan, 8th June, 1859."

Much as Napoleon III. had accomplished with
the allied forces under his command, in victories
in the field, and in the occupation of the capital,
much still remained to be done to complete the
final expulsion of the Austrians from Italy. A
portion of their retreating forces, in crossing the
plain of Lombardy towards the line of the Mincio,
the boundary stream between Italian and Austrian
territory, turned to make a stand at Melegnano,
a town four leagues S.E. from Milan, about mid-
way between that city and Lodi. They occupied
the place in strength, with the object of protecting
the passage of their main army across the river
Adda. On the 8th of June, Marshal Baraguey
d'Hilliers received the order to attack their position with the 1st corps; taking also with him the
2nd corps, commanded by Marshal Mac-Mahon.
On the evening of that day, the Austrians, after a
gallant resistance on their part of three hours,

were driven from the town with severe loss, leaving about 2,000 prisoners, of whom 1,200 were wounded, in the hands of their antagonists. The losses of the French, in killed and wounded, are stated in the official report of Baraguey d'Hilliers as 943, of whom 69 were officers.

After two days' rest in and near Milan, the French and Sardinians were again in motion, to follow up their enemy in his retreat on the Mincio. On the morning of the 11th of June, the 1st, 2nd, 3rd, and 4th corps d'armée commenced their march in that direction; the troops of Victor Emmanuel taking a more northerly route towards the same destination. On the 12th the Emperor followed, with the Imperial Guard as the reserve. He had decided that the army should march by Brescia, though the route lay through a tract hilly and rugged in many places, and, in its more cultivated portions, crossed by frequent canals of irrigation and considerable water-courses. In choosing this intricate line of march the Emperor observed the policy which had before guided his operations, of turning, rather than attacking, fortified posts held by his adversary. The French army reached Brescia from Milan in eight days (on the 18th June), without having encountered any opposition. The Emperor was welcomed by the inhabitants of the city with hearty acclamations, and fixed his head-quarters there during the 19th and 20th. His troops required such a term of repose from their fatigues ; and he employed the interval in summoning (on the evening of the 19th) the chiefs of the several corps, together with the commanding officers of the engineers and artillery, to a council of war.

" The conjuncture was one which called for anxious deliberation. The success which had hitherto attended the French and Sardinian troops impressed them indeed with confidence of future victory ; and a courageous energy pervaded all ranks, increasing as their foe continued to retire before them. But that foe had already received large reinforcements from the garrisons of Mantua, Peschiera, and Verona ; and was falling back on the resources of a mighty empire ; while the allies, on the contrary, were daily departing farther from their original base of operations and sources of supply. It was not likely that the Austrians would abandon Lombardy without striking another blow for so fair a land ; and they might be expected to concentrate their forces for a decisive effort. On the three days' march from Brescia to the Mincio, much of the road lay over vast plains, as those near Montechiaro and Castiglione ; bare of all obstacles to the operations of cavalry, an arm hitherto little brought into action during the campaign, and on which Austria placed great reliance. Was it not probable that she would select this as a field for another battle, which any hour might bring on ? On the 23rd of June, however, when approaching the river, the Emperor received certain intelligence that the whole Austrian army had crossed it two days previously; thus forsaking formidable positions afforded by the range of heights extending parallel to its right bank, from the Lago di Garda in a S.E. direction as far as to Volta. There remained no vestige of warlike array along the borders of the Mincio ; the eye discerned only the low line of trees marking the course of the stream, and the blue mist rising from the sedgy banks :

> Propter aquam tardis ingens ubi fluctibus errat
> Mincius, et tenera prætexit arundine ripas.*

But the scene was quickly to undergo a terrible

* Virg. Georg. lib. iii. v. 14.

change. It had been doubted whether the Austrians would dispute the passage of the river by their pursuers, or retire further within shelter of their famed "Quadrilateral," guarded at its four angles by the almost impregnable fortresses of Peschiera, Verona, Mantua, and Legnano. But it was little anticipated that, having once crossed the stream, they would retrace their steps and resume the offensive on Italian soil. Such, however, was the plan which they adopted. On the night of the 23rd they re-crossed the Mincio, and proceeded to re-occupy the heights which they had abandoned on the 21st. At the same hour, the allied armies, from the opposite side, were advancing to occupy the same heights. The adverse hosts were thus approaching to a collision, each equally unaware of the movement of the other. The Emperor, to spare his troops the inconvenience of toiling through the torrid heat of a midsummer day, had issued orders to the several corps of his army to commence their march two hours after midnight. The Sardinians, who formed the northern extremity of the allied line at Lonato, near to the Lago di Garda, began their march at an early hour, in the direction of

188 LIFE OF NAPOLEON III.

Peschiera and Pozzolongo. They encountered the
Austrian advanced posts, and drove them in ; but
were in turn obliged to retire before a superior
force. Reinforcements coming up on both sides
maintained a series of combats with alternate
success, resulting finally to the advantage of the
Sardinians.

The 1st French corps d'armée, under command
of Baraguey d'Hilliers, advancing at 2 a.m. on
Solferino, in the centre of the line, soon became
engaged with the light troops of the enemy ; and,
having succeeded, after various severe combats, in
making its way to the foot of the Solferino hill,
found the Austrians established strongly there, in
the village, and in the fortified heights which
overlook it.

At the same time, the 2nd corps (Mac-Mahon),
encountering in its progress large masses of
Austrian troops, was precluded, by the necessity
of repelling their attacks, from proceeding to the
support of the 1st corps. The 3rd and 4th,
(Canrobert and Niel), too far asunder from each
other for mutual support, were in like manner
severally engaged against strong hostile columns.

Thus, along a battle front extending twelve

miles, the morning of the 24th broke on 300,000 men closing in deadly conflict.

The Emperor was at Montechiaro. He had despatched the infantry of the Guard to Castiglione, at five o'clock, and fixed a later hour for the departure of the cavalry. At half past five, two horsemen, arriving at full speed, galloped into the encampment. They were aides-de-camp of the Marshals Baraguey d' Hilliers and Mac-Mahon, sent to inform the Emperor that they had joined battle with the Austrians, who covered the hill of Solferino and adjacent heights, and extended to a considerable distance both on the right and left. The Emperor, in consequence, accelerated the departure of the cavalry, and repaired with his staff to Castiglione. From its summit he was enabled to obtain a general view of the battle-field. The survey determined him, without hesitation, at that early stage of the battle, to bring his reserve into action. Proceeding to Marshal Mac-Mahon, he placed at his disposal the cavalry of the Guard, and then hastened on to the centre, where Baraguey d'Hilliers had sustained for several hours an unequal contest against the main force of the Austrian army. The veteran Marshal, whose head was blanched by the campaigns of forty years, mingled in the thickest of the fray, encouraging and leading his troops, by voice and example, to the charge. French and Austrians by turns gave or gained ground, but with no decisive result. When one regiment retired, shattered and exhausted, another filled immediately its place, and the combat was renewed with fresh fury. No quarter was given, or asked, during that terrible struggle, nor had the officers always the power to restrain the soldiers from wreaking their rage on the wounded and fallen. The French, worn out by the heat and fatigue, and decimated by a heavy fire, gained ground with much difficulty against forces incessantly renewed. While the event of the strife hung thus doubtful, a shout rising from all the French ranks announced the arrival of the Emperor. The presence of their Commander-in-chief inspired the troops with an ardour which overcame all obstacles; and the orders which he issued exercised a speedy influence on the fortunes of the day. After examining the strength of the situation occupied by the enemy, whose shot and shell fell fast and thick around him, the Emperor ordered the advance of the 3rd division of the 1st corps, under command of General Forey, and supported it by the light division of the Imperial Guard ; directing at the same moment a battery of artillery of the Guard to take a position close to the hostile entrenchments. This manœuvre decided the success of the attack on the centre, and the gain of the battle. The divisions of the 1st corps dashed forward and seized the village and cemetery; while the Guard, climbing the steep height above, possessed themselves of the ancient fortifications and tower which command the site. The Austrians offered still a brave resistance at various points, incited by the presence of their Emperor Francis Joseph, who, from a hill behind Solferino, witnessed the result of the conflict. The heights were successively carried, and, at the close of the day, the Austrians finally retreated from the position, under a fire of artillery from the French, leaving in their hands 1500 prisoners, 14 pieces of cannon, and 2 colours.

The Austrians, after their defeat at Solferino, abandoned entirely the line of the Mincio ; and on the 1st of July the whole of the allied armies had passed to the left side of that river. In the midst, however, of these uninterrupted successes, Europe was surprised suddenly to hear that an interview had taken place between the two Emperors at Villafranca, and that an armistice was agreed upon. This was soon followed by a treaty of peace, signed at Villafranca on the 11th of July. The Emperor Napoleon has himself assigned as a main reason for the conduct which he thus adopted, that to have pushed his triumphs further against Austria would have provoked a collision with the whole Germanic Confederation, and put him under the necessity of "accepting a combat on the Rhine." To this he added, in his reply to the address of congratulation from the diplomatic body at Paris on the 19th of July : "Europe was in general so unjust towards me at the commencement of the war, that I was happy to be able to conclude peace as soon as the honour and interests of France were satisfied."

On the whole, it will be generally admitted that France had sufficient grounds to be contented with the measure of success that crowned her efforts in the campaign of 1859. Seven years later, the Italians exulted in the complete attainment of the objects for which the war was undertaken. Of the two alternatives proposed at its commencement : " whether Austria should extend her despotism as far as to the Alps, or Italy be free to the Adriatic :" the latter has finally prevailed.

CHAPTER VIII.

THE EMPEROR AND THE PEOPLE.

"Look for your friends among the commons ever."
Philip Van Artevelde, Act i. sc. 4.

THE Emperor has said : " My friends are found
not only in palaces, but also beneath roofs of
thatch, and in the cottages of the poor." The
attachment of all ranks is obviously essential to a
sovereign whose rule is based upon the national
will; and France has never been deficient in
testifying, by proofs stronger than mere words
could convey, whenever occasion required, her
affection towards the " Chief of her choice."*
It is quite impossible that Napoleon III. could
have retained for twenty years and upwards so
unvarying a hold on the hearts and minds of
Frenchmen, except through their conviction of

* " There are links that must break in the chain which hath
bound us,
Then turn thee and call on the Chief of thy choice."
" *Napoleon's Farewell*," Byron.

his being more than even a wise ruler and brave leader :—

"Plus que brave soldat, plus que grand capitaine,"

a just also and a beneficent sovereign.

It may be presumed that no one will pretend to account for the constancy of attachment shewn by the French people to Louis Napoleon on the hypothesis that the temper of the popular masses is less fickle in France than in other countries. I am tempted to adduce an instance to the contrary. There is in Paris a particular quarter which has never been renowned for submission to lawful authority; and has at times evinced a decided bias to revolt; the Faubourg Saint Antoine. Its population, however, is not of a criminal, but rather of an industrial character; inured to hard work, rough in manners and usages. It happened that the Prince Louis Napoleon, during the time of his Presidency, rode one morning through the main street of the Faubourg, on his road to Vincennes. He was recognised. Groups of sinister and hostile visages collected around his path, and, increasing in numbers, awaited his return. As their demeanour bore no good augury, a message was speedily conveyed to Vincennes to the effect that, in consequence of the threatening aspect of affairs, it would be prudent to avoid the Faubourg Saint Antoine, and re-enter Paris by some other way. The Prince, however, had a different apprehension of the conduct which became him. Returning in the evening, at the hour previously appointed, as he approached the formidable Faubourg, he desired his escort to remain at a long distance behind him, and rode alone at a slow pace into the midst of the quarter, over the very ground which had been reddened, a few months before, by the blood of the Archbishop of Paris. The assemblage maintained at first an ominous silence : gradually, however, the confidence of the Prince produced the effect which a display of cool courage usually has on the multitude: " *Au moins, il n'a pas peur, celui-là.*" " *Tiens, c'est un gaillard avec lequel il ne ferait pas bon badiner:*" such were the remarks heard, with others more emphatic than elegant. At length, as if moved by a single sudden impulse, the vast crowd burst forth into a shout loud and prolonged : " *Vive M. le President.*"

It is true that the sentiments expressed in other countries of Europe have, at various times, responded but ill to those held generally in France respecting Louis Napoleon. The suspicion and distrust which foreign Governments have cast on his policy, and their misconstruction of his motives, have drawn from him remonstrance and reproof on more than one occasion. Thus, in a letter dated St. Cloud, 29th of July, 1860, to Count Persigny, the French Ambassador at London, we find the following sentence: "Au nom du ciel, que les hommes éminents placés à la tête du Gouvernement Anglais laissent de côté des jalousies mesquines et des défiances injustes. Entendons-nous loyalement, comme d'honnêtes gens que nous sommes, et non comme des larrons qui veulent se duper réciproquement."

In addition to the heavier toils and cares which attend high office, its possessor is exposed, by a rule which admits no exception, to the cavils and misrepresentations of prejudice and jealousy. "The honours of this world," the Emperor wrote, not long since, to a French cardinal,* "are a heavy burden imposed on us by Providence, who in justice augments our duties in proportion to our dignities. Thus, I often ask myself if in prosperity our

* Cardinal Bonnechose.

troubles are not as great as in adversity. Our guide and support is faith, religious faith and political, in other words, confidence in God, and consciousness of a mission to accomplish." " Notre guide et notre soutien, c'est la foi, la foi religieuse, et la foi politique : c'est à dire, la confiance en Dieu, et la conscience d'une mission à accomplir."

In reviewing the eventful career of Napoleon III. we perceive most prominently at every stage of it, as well in his prison at Ham and as on his throne at the Tuileries, alike in the vicissitudes of peace and war, the same constant expression of trust in Providence, the same acknowledgment of the " Sovereign Commander of all the world," who decrees the issue of battles, the establishment or downfall of dynasties. On the eve of his departure on his Italian campaign, in 1859, the Emperor thus addressed his chaplains assembled at the Tuileries : " Priez pour moi ; j'ai une belle et brave armée, mais je compte encore plus sur le secours de Dieu, et de vos prières."* It was an example worthy the head of a Christian nation, when, on intelligence of the capture of Sebastopol, he repaired to the Cathedral Church of Notre

* Mullois.

Dame de Paris (13 September, 1855), to render thanks to the only Giver of all victory. Being met at the door by the Archbishop, Napoleon III. declared : " I am come here, Monseigneur, to thank heaven for the triumph granted to our arms, for I am glad to acknowledge that in spite of the skill of generals, and the valour of soldiers, nothing can succeed without the protection of Providence." "Je viens ici, Monseigneur, remercier le ciel du triomphe qu'il a accordé à nos armes, car je me plais à reconnaître que, malgré l'habilité des généraux et le courage des soldats, rien ne peut réussir sans la protection de la Providence." It has been justly remarked : " L'Empereur a si souvent rencontré la Providence sur son chemin dans la vie qu'il ne lui a pas été possible de la méconnaître." There are, of course, and have ever been, persons who scoff at the belief in the Almighty Ruler and Disposer of events, and who hold, with the " Roi philosophe " of Prussia, that " le bon Dieu est toujours du côté des gros bataillons," but no one truly great or wise can be of their number :

> " For of such doctrine never was there school,
> Save the heart of the fool."

In referring his title to empire, under Providence as supreme, to the national will as declared in his favour by the free and general suffrage of the French people, Louis Napoleon adhered, as in other points of his career, to the model of his early aspirations, in the character and actions of Napoleon I. The time has long gone by when that name excited in England the wildest feelings and bitterest expressions of national antipathy. At a Social Science Congress held at Liverpool in October, 1858, Earl Russell, then Lord John Russell, spoke in the following terms respecting the founder of the Napoleon dynasty. The orator, it will be seen, warms into eloquence on his theme :

" At the beginning of the present century, the First Consul of France had attained the fame of a great military commander. In his wonderful Italian campaigns he had defeated the most experienced generals of Austria. He had recently seized the reins of power which had fallen from the feeble hands of his predecessor. He had subdued and tamed the remnants of the Jacobin faction, which was still thirsting for blood. He had opened the ports of France to the partisans

of the ancient monarchy, who were still panting
for a restoration. *It was his aim to restore peace to
society, to give to religion her altars, to replace justice
in her sanctuary.* In the midst of these labours
he determined to bestow on France a simple and
enlightened code of laws. For this purpose he
assembled a Council, in which the learned
civilians of the days of Louis XVI. sat by the
side of the able lawyers of the regicide convention. There, after the morning inspection of his
troops, he would sit from twelve o'clock at noon
till five in the afternoon, never inattentive, never
weary, marking out clearly, without passion and
without prejudice, the best foundation on which
property, marriage, commerce, in short, all the
complicated relations of life itself, were thereafter
to repose. In discussion, the opinion of the
ablest civilian, and not that of the military
dictator, generally prevailed. When the work
had been for some time proceeded with, it was
sent to all the legal tribunals of France, with a
request that any remarks which the Judges might
have to make should be transmitted to Paris.
Thus debated, discussed, draughted, corrected,
augmented and revised, the Code Napoléon, in its

different portions, was´ published, at intervals extending over seven years, as the law of France.

"And now, what is the result? The splendid victories of Napoleon, the rush of armies, the roar of cannon, the masterly decision, the instant obedience, have passed away. The pride of empire, the kings waiting in the ante-chamber, the sway of a mighty will from Rome to Hamburgh, from the Manzanares to the Elbe, has vanished like the baseless fabric of a vision. But the transactions between man and man, the trial of the offender, the adjudication of property throughout the French Empire, are still regulated, and probably will long be regulated, by the statutes of the immortal legislator."

It will be generally acknowledged that higher praise has seldom been bestowed by man on man than the above eulogy pronounced by Earl Russell on the First Great Napoleon. Napoleon III., following the example of his predecessor, has rescued France, (to cite the phrase of M. de Montalembert)* from "the gaping gulf of victorious socialism." No other might than that of

* See ante, p. 95.

God can thus, in the crisis of danger, endue an individual with powers, not given in the ordinary course of Providence, to raise a nation from anarchy and abasement to independence and honour.

> " A nobler aim, a purer law,
>   Nor priest, nor bard, nor sage, has taught."

(205)

INDEX.

A.

AFRICAN SLAVE TRADE, essay on, by Louis Napoleon, 38.
ARCHBISHOP OF PARIS, murder of, 61.

B.

BALLOT, for the Presidency of the Republic, 65 ;—for the
same with extended powers, 96 ;—for re-establishment
of the Imperial dynasty, 123.
BARAGUEY D'HILLIERS, Marshal, commanding the 1st *Corps
d'armée ;* his perilous position at the battle of Solférino,
190.
BERRYER, M. de, speech of, in defence of Louis Napoleon, on
his trial before the Chamber of Peers, 24.
BILLAULT, M., speech of, on reporting to Louis Napoleon his
election as Emperor, 123.
BONNECHOSE, Cardinal, saying addressed to, by the Emperor,
197.
BORDEAUX, speech of Louis Napoleon to the Chamber of
Commerce, 119.
BOULOGNE, expedition to, 23.
BREA, General, murder of, 60.
BROGLIE, Duc de, his opinion of the Constitution made by
the National Assembly, November, 1848, 75.
BUFFALORA, bridge of, held against superior numbers, by a
division of the Guard, under command of the Emperor
176.

H.

I.

L.

M.

N.

London. SWIFT & Co., King Street, Regent Street, W.